HIS TO RAVAGE

EMILY HALE

HIS TO RAVAGE

CHAPTER ONE

I *can't keep screwing up like this.*
It didn't help to beat herself up over something that was over and done with, but Kimani had never been in a situation like this before. She was supposed to be working—undercover. Which meant that she had to be extra careful not to compromise the story or its subjects. And her own journalistic integrity.

What had she done instead?

Become sexually involved with one of the subjects. And not just any subject. Beside her in the driver's seat of the Jeep Wrangler sat the son of one of the wealthiest families in the world. When he took over the family business, Benjamin Dmitri Lee would be worth somewhere in the vicinity of twelve billion dollars.

Her editor, Sam Green, hadn't wasted any time. With the bits of information she had provided him last night—an Asian named Ben who went to Howard University, then the Stanford business school, and was recruiting for a team in the Chinese Basketball Association—he had come back with the Lee Family Corporation. Ben's father, Lee Hua Jing, had founded the Lee Family Corporation, making his first million in residential real estate before branching into commercial real estate and investments of all kinds. Mr. Lee's younger brother, Gordon, had immigrated to the United States as a teenager when the family was still struggling to make ends meet, and was now in a tightly contested election for mayor of Oakland. And one of the hot button issues in the election was the development of a piece of waterfront property that the Lee Family Corporation had acquired.

"This could be a great scoop," Sam had said. "You've got to find out more."

But Benjamin Lee was a tangent. A tall, sexy tangent, whose sensuous touch had a way of shutting down her brain. Even now, she tried not to glance over to admire how his simple shirt fit luxuriously over his broad shoulders and chiseled chest. She supposed this was a side effect of not having had sex in the last six months because she was focused on her career, trying to land a job with the *San Francisco Tribune.*

She was supposed to be reporting on the Scarlet Auction, where women sold themselves for a week to the highest bidder. Undercover, Kimani had participated in the auction with the intent of exposing its sordid business. Ben hadn't attended the actual auction, but he had "bought" her from the man, a sports agent named Jake, who had won her with a bid of thirty thousand dollars.

It was crazy shit that had boggled her mind. Jake's first purchase, a blond virgin named Claire, had "sold" for eighty thousand dollars. But crazy went through the stratosphere when Ben offered Jake two hundred thousand dollars for Kimani.

Kimani couldn't fathom why he would shell out that kind of money for her unless, (a) two hundred thousand dollars was just the equivalent of a pricey vacation and he could easily make the amount back if the HKEX had a good run; (b) Ben didn't want to be the only guy in the group without a date— correction: fucktoy; or (c) Ben was messed up in the head.

But he didn't seem irrational or deranged.

In fact, out of all the people she was stuck in a lakeside cabin in the boonies of Northern California with, he seemed the most calm and collected. Even now, when they had been driving in silence for several minutes, she could sense him looking at her, at ease with their silence, probably wondering what she was thinking but restrained enough not to ask.

Her American-style impatience got the better of her, however, and she turned to ask him, "Where are we going?"

For a second, she wondered if psychos had the capability of appearing completely normal. He had put the top down on the Jeep Wrangler, and if he had intended to drive her somewhere with evil intentions, he wouldn't have wanted himself and his victim to be so visible, right? Then again, they were in one of the least-populated counties in the state. Trinity County was mostly rugged, heavily forested wilderness.

"We're going into Weaverville to get you some clothes," he replied.

His answer surprised her. This morning he had made her go onto Jake's boat without a shred of clothing. Afterwards, he'd allowed her to put on her cocktail dress, her only clothing item, with his shirt over it. She hadn't had a chance to wash the sweats he'd lent her.

Remembering that she didn't have on panties, she pressed her legs together.

"I don't have any money with me," she said. Her cellphone and wallet had disappeared from her handbag sometime during the auction, before she'd been ushered into a limo that had driven her and Claire straight to Jake's cabin. Ben had let her use his cellphone twice, and it was her only connection to the rest of the world. Sam knew she was somewhere near Weaverville because that's all *she* knew. And that probably wasn't going to be helpful if things turned ugly.

"You don't need any money."

"Oh. I'll pay you back when we get back to San Francisco."

"When" we get back. Not "if." She'd had her worries yesterday, especially after Jake had hit her before Ben had arrived. Ben had been her savior, buying her from Jake, because the thought of laying a finger on Jake made her want to retch. Even though she barely knew him, she felt safer with Ben.

Relatively safer, she cautioned herself.

Ben had an edge. She could see it when his pupils constricted and his jaw tightened. Beneath that cool exterior lay a tiger. He kept a good leash on it, but she couldn't be sure what would set it off.

"I've got it," he said.

"I'd rather pay you back."

"Maybe if you're good, I'll let you pay me back."

She bristled at this "good" business, like she was a little girl. But it was better than being called "Slut #2," Jake's original moniker for her, but not that much better.

"I insist."

He glanced at her as if she were a child who wanted to have cookies before bed. "You don't get to make the rules, pet."

She bristled again. "Then maybe I don't want to get any clothes."

As soon as the words escaped her mouth, she regretted her childish response. It was an outright lie. She wanted something other than her cocktail dress and clothes borrowed from him, even though his shirt and sweatpants were the softest things she had ever worn. She wanted underwear. Desperately. Having a shield of any kind down there might keep those carnal instincts from running away with her better judgment.

She had said what she said because she wanted some small sliver of control, and she didn't want to be beholden to Ben more than she already was.

But Ben granted her no concessions. "You're welcome to go naked the whole week."

Then maybe I don't want to stay the whole week.

This time, she curbed herself from saying anything rash. Ben had said he wasn't going to force her to stay, and had even offered to fly her back to San Francisco in his jet if she wanted. He had sounded sincere. But she didn't have enough material for her story. And she couldn't abandon Claire to Jake. He might be as bad as the man who had beaten up Kimani's roommate, Marissa. And by exposing the Scarlet Auction, Kimani hoped to prevent another woman from getting beaten up or taken advantage of.

"I'll find a way to pay you back," Kimani decided aloud. Maybe she'd make a donation in his name to the ACLU or the local Black Women's Political Caucus. Maybe then he'd prefer to take her money.

He gave her an amused look but said nothing as they neared Weaverville. With the

Trinity Alps as its backdrop, Weaverville was a picturesque Gold Rush town. Though the last census pegged the population at less than four thousand people, Main Street looked busy, probably from the influx of tourists taking advantage of the area's outdoor sports offerings.

The clothing retail options were limited, but Ben found a thrift store to park in front of. He left her alone to peruse the clothing racks. She found a tank top, t-shirt, a long knit skirt that went almost to her ankles, a pair of khaki shorts, a sports bra, flip-flops, a silk scarf to tie her hair up at night, and cheap sunglasses so that she could return Ben's Louis Vuitton shades. She also picked out a dress for Claire, whom she had been whisked to the cabin with, without a chance to pack.

At the checkout, Ben had a few items to purchase as well: boxed candles and several neckties. She wondered why he would need business attire at the cabin.

Eager to be out of her heels and strange ensemble, she changed into the shirt, shorts and flip-flops and immediately felt better. Now she only needed underwear.

As if reading her mind, Ben said, "There's

a CVS store about a mile down."

"Can we walk?" she asked. The summer sun shone warmly, and she preferred taking in the downtown scenery, with its many nineteenth century buildings, to going back to the cabin where Jake and his buddies were.

After putting their purchase in the car, they started walking down Main Street. She had never been in this part of the state before. Her eyes lit upon seeing a sign for the Joss House State Historic Park.

" You want to check it out?" Ben didn't miss much.

"Definitely!"

While on Jake's boat earlier today, upset that Ben had made her go naked like the other three women, she had insinuated he was an asshole. But moments like this showed he couldn't be a complete asshole. This, and the fact that he had let her take a nap in his room yesterday afternoon, and had looked upset to see the basement where Jake had her and the other women sleep. Ben had made sure she and Claire had something to eat when they were hungry after Jake made them kneel on the floor for three hours.

And, despite having made her come twice

yesterday and once today, he had yet to demand she return the favor. He'd made no bones about the fact that he had purchased her for sex, so why hadn't he made her do anything to him? Maybe he was embarrassed about his size down there? Somehow, she doubted that was what was holding him back. When she felt more generously inclined toward him, she thought perhaps he just wanted to make her comfortable. But surely that was giving him too much credit? After all, he had paid money—a ridiculous amount of money—for sex. He couldn't be that different from the other overgrown frat boys, Jake, Derek, and Jason.

Turning the corner, they came upon a quaint red building. Built in 1874 and dubbed "The Temple of the Forest Beneath the Clouds," the Weaverville Joss House was the oldest Chinese Temple in California. Weaverville was once home to some 2,000 Chinese gold miners. Many Chinese immigrants came to California in the nineteenth century for the state's famed Gold Rush or to work as laborers on the transcontinental railroad. Their large numbers caused Congress to pass the Chinese Exclusion Act, the only US law ever to prevent immigration and naturalization on the basis of race.

The interior housed displays of art, pictures, mining tools and weapons used in the 1854 Tong War.

"A friend of mine carried a small hatchet similar to this one," said Ben, almost to himself.

"Why would he carry around a hatchet?" Kimani asked.

"He was old-fashioned. Didn't like guns because they were a Western invention."

"Gunpowder was a Chinese invention, though I guess it was the Europeans who first used it for mass destruction and guns. Was your friend extremely paranoid? Or was carrying around a hatchet some kind of alpha-guy thing?"

"Chen Kai wasn't more paranoid than the rest of us."

"Rest of us?"

"When I was young, and my father was busy taking the family business to the next level, I started getting into gangs. That's why he shipped me off to boarding school in London."

"Were you pretty deep in a gang?"

"I didn't kill anyone if that's what you're

worried about."

It *was* sort of what worried her. "So what did you do in the gang?"

"Not much since I was still pretty young at the time. Stupid boy shit. Probably got myself beat up more than anything else."

She had a hard time imagining anyone beating up on Ben. She saw how he moved. Smooth like a ballerina, flowing like one of those dragons in the Chinese New Year's Parade. She'd seen him in nothing but his swim trunks. His muscles were well defined everywhere, not in a beefy way but plenty delicious for her to want to run her hands over the planes and ridges of his chest and torso.

"Did you have to carry a weapon?" she asked.

"I carried a knife and learned how to make *myself* a weapon through martial arts. The gang was small potatoes, only loosely connected to one of the triads, but enough to worry my dad."

She itched to ask him a dozen questions, which she would have done if she were openly interviewing him, but since she wasn't, everything was technically off record. She wanted to know anyway but didn't want to appear prying.

They walked to the area of worship.

"This is so cool," she whispered of the paper prayers on the walls and intricately carved altars decorated with bold colors of red and gold. "It's not something I expected to find out here."

She looked at one of the scrolls hanging from beside the altar. "Do you read?"

After he had translated the Chinese on the scrolls, which talked of the emperor, gods, and devils, she recalled, "One of my dormmates at Stanford claimed to be a Taoist, but he only talked about it in reference to sex. I'm not sure how authentic it all was. Some people thought he was just being an egg."

She glanced at him—and it was like walking into a brick wall when she met his stare. At first, she thought maybe he didn't like that she had used the term "egg," since it was sometimes used in a critical manner to refer to white Asiaphiles, but there was an amused gleam in Ben's dark brown eyes that told her he was fixed on *her*, not her words.

She could barely swallow. He looked as if he had some secret he may or may not share with her. She wanted to know what it was, even though she was certain that finding out would only get her deeper in trouble.

CHAPTER TWO

By her expression, not unlike a deer caught in headlights, Ben supposed he must have been staring at Kimani like she was a piece of meat he wanted to devour. And he did. On the drive over to Weaverville, he had toyed with the idea of pulling over and making her come all over the car. He was going to make her squirt again, just like he had the night before. The morning swim through the lake's cold waters had helped clear his head, but spending all that time on the boat and seeing her naked had put him back to square one. Her body had felt so bloody good leaning against his.

She stood inches from him, looking like a frumpy tourist with her broad-brimmed hat, cheap sunglasses, and khaki shorts. And if there had been no one around, he would have been tempted to rip her clothes off and take her right there in the temple. Or at least feel her up through the thin tank top she wore. He had noticed she had chosen a sports bra, which made her breasts less accessible, but she was wrong if she thought a little sports bra could protect her.

"Sex is an important part of Taoism," he explained, "and some engage in intercourse as part of a spiritual practice."

"Really? Sex is usually taboo and *wrong* when it comes to religions."

"Taoism isn't a religion in the same way as Catholicism or Judaism. It's a philosophy and a way of living. Central to Taoist practice is the care and cultivation of *jing*, essence or energy. Sex is the joining of this energy."

She was eying him curiously, as if trying to read his mind. If she could, she would see herself spent and exhausted as he wrung yet another orgasm from her. She had no idea how long a session with him could last. Most women couldn't keep up, and he wondered how Kimani would fare compared to the others.

"That sounds very holistic, spiritual," she commented. Then, as if sensing his thoughts, though she couldn't see them, she turned and stepped away. "Looks like there's a garden out back."

A deer leaped over the fence as they strolled outside to a fountain with a small statue of Kuan Yin.

"'One who listens,'" Kimani read from the plaque in front of the fountain. "Is she a goddess?"

"Sort of. She's an enlightenment being, and the gateway to a paradise where souls are reborn with the truth of their eternal nature, compassion and joy."

"That sounds lovely. You seem to know quite a bit about Taoism."

He didn't tell her that it was the Taoist sex practices that had been his primary interest. It was best to stay away from topics of a sexual nature. Any wood would show in his tight-fitting jeans.

Instead, he said, "Taoism is embedded in Chinese culture, though much of it was suppressed in favor of Confucianism."

After they finished their visit at the Joss House, he decided to stop in one of the coffee shops to get something to drink. He wanted Kimani to himself and was in no hurry to get back to the cabin where his cousin, Jason, was probably getting stoned with Tweedledee and Tweedledum. The three of them had tried to convince him to attend the Scarlet Auction to "buy" a woman for the week. He had thought the idea of buying a woman stupid— for guys too lazy to get real dates.

But the instant he saw Kimani, he had to have her. Or at least he couldn't let Jake keep her, especially if he was the one who had given her the bruise on her cheek, which had deepened in hue since yesterday.

If it weren't for the fact Jake Whitehurst represented players that the coach of the Golden Phoenix wanted to recruit to play in the Chinese Basketball Association, Ben would not have chosen to spend the week in the wilderness of Northern California. But Kimani was going to make it all worthwhile.

At the coffee shop, he ordered two mugs of green tea.

"Green tea?" Kimani echoed in disbelief. "It's warm out here. I was hoping to get an iced mocha."

"Green tea is healthier."

"So is broccoli juice, but that doesn't mean I want to drink it."

Should he tell her that green tea enhanced *physical performance* or would that scare her off?

"Do you only do what you want?" he returned, taking the mugs of tea from the barista.

She followed him to a table. "Of course not. I'm not a child. But...green tea? *Hot* green tea on a sunny afternoon?"

"You'll get used to it."

She gave him a dubious look as she sat down. He almost laughed when she grimaced into her tea.

"You can have a glass of water after you've had some of your tea," he said.

She blew at the tea to cool it down. "You're obnoxious."

"We established earlier that I was an asshole," he acknowledged before leaning in and lowering his voice. "You came for me anyway."

She flushed. "Well, that's because you're not a *complete* asshole. Just partly. Maybe a majority. I haven't decided yet."

He leaned back in his chair with his tea. She was cute when she was flustered. He knew her type: smart, well-educated, a little arrogant. But she had enough humility inside of her that if she were knocked down from her high horse, she would get up stronger and wiser.

"So do you work for the Chinese Basketball Association?" she asked.

"You haven't had any of your tea yet," he told her.

She took a sip. "Is that why you're doing business with Jake?"

He nodded at her tea. "Drink more."

She took another sip. "So do you?"

"Why are you so interested?"

"Curious. I used to play," she reminded him. "A part of me wishes I was good enough to play professionally."

"How do you know you aren't?"

"I guess if I had stuck with it, one never knows. But when I was applying to college, it wasn't clear what options I would have playing ball. But I like what I'm doing now."

He raised a brow. "Working as an office assistant?"

She looked down. Shoot. She forgot that was what she had provided as her cover. "I know that's not what most Stanford grads aspire to, but it pays the bills."

"Does it? You wouldn't have done the Scarlet Auction if you had enough money."

"Right. I meant my job pays most of the bills. The Scarlet Auction is a great opportunity to make extra cash to pay off student loans and maybe have some fun."

"What does 'fun' entail?"

"Getting tickets to a Warriors game."

"Is that your favorite team?"

"The Stanford women's team is my favorite team, but the Warriors are a close second." She was smiling and looking more relaxed. She even took another sip of tea without prompting. "You didn't answer my question about working for the CBA."

"I don't work for the CBA. My father sponsors the Golden Phoenix, and it's his pet project to make the team into a championship contender."

"So when you're not working on that, what do you do?"

"Mostly real estate developments for the family business."

"Any here in California?"

"Some."

"Like in the Bay Area?"

"Some."

He set down his now empty mug. Unlike most dates, she seemed interested in details. But this wasn't a date, even though it was beginning to feel like one. He didn't date because he wasn't looking to start a family.

"Are they commercial or residential?"

"These days, policymakers like to see mixed use for urban areas."

"Do you like mixed use?"

"If the pro forma works, sure. Mixed use is key to smart growth principles."

Her brows went up. "You care about smart growth?"

"Why shouldn't I?"

"I thought..."

"Thought what? That developers are evil and have no conscience when it comes to the environment? That we just care about maxing returns and triple net?"

"What's triple net?"

"It's a lease agreement in which the tenant agrees to pay the three 'nets' on the property: taxes, insurance and maintenance."

She seemed to be storing away that bit of information. He was surprised to find himself talking about lease agreements with any woman who wasn't in the business, but he suspected few subjects would intimidate Kimani. And he found he talked rather freely with her. Hell, he had even revealed he had once hung with a gang. He couldn't remember the last person he had told that to.

After the coffee shop, they walked to the drugstore, where she found a package of Hanes underwear, various hair products, toiletries, a notepad, and pens.

"I'll pay you back," she said as the cashier rang everything up.

"I got it," he reminded her.

"I'd rather pay you back. It's all stuff I would have needed at home anyway."

He studied her, wondering why she insisted on paying him back when she was financially desperate enough to participate in the Scarlet Auction.

"You'll pay me back," he assured her, "just not in the way you think."

CHAPTER THREE

"How much longer before we get to the cabin?" she asked after they'd been driving a while. The top of the Jeep was back on, making the space of the vehicle feel smaller.

"About thirty-five minutes."

She frowned and squirmed in her seat. That was too long to have to hold it. "I shouldn't have had that tea."

He looked her over, as if he could assess how badly she needed to go. "I can pull over."

The thought of having to go on the side of the road apparently didn't appeal to her. "Let's just see how it goes."

"You could masturbate."

"What? I need to pee, not get off."

"Getting off will distract you from the urge to piss."

"No thanks. I don't want to have an accident in this car."

"Do it. Masturbate."

"Are you serious?"

"Yes."

When she didn't move, he took a hand off the steering wheel. "You want me to do it for you?"

"No, no. I'd rather you focus on driving."

He didn't say anything, but there was no way in hell he could focus all of his attention on driving with her masturbating next to him.

"I'll just go on the side of the road. There's a clearing up ahead that you can pull into."

"I'll pull over after you've masturbated."

Her mouth fell open. She ought to stop doing that. She had no idea how sexy she looked when she did that. He wanted to pull over, but not so she could do her business.

"You're joking, right?" she asked.

"Nope."

She crossed her arms. "You just being an asshole then?"

"Yep."

He could tell his answers annoyed her. "It's not like you haven't masturbated for me. You did a damn good job on the boat this morning."

"If you don't pull over, I'm going to have an accident in the car."

"Don't make a threat you can't follow through on."

This seemed to annoy her the most. She glared at him with open hostility.

"You can make this a lot easier on yourself if you don't fight me. I might reward you for being good by being less of an asshole."

Her hostility flared even more because she knew she was stuck between a rock and a hard place. She didn't want to cede control, but she didn't want to provoke his assholeness more. He knew she wouldn't risk pissing in the car.

"I hope you're right about this," she grumbled ruefully as she undid the button of her shorts. She pushed a hand down between those delicious thighs of hers.

Closing his eyes for a second, he imagined her hand at her snatch. Maybe he would take his shaver to her down there. Just to mark her further as his.

"What are you doing?"

"What do you think I'm doing?" she spat.

"I want to *see* what you're doing, but since I've got to keep my eyes on the road, you're going to have to tell me."

She gave him a "you're such an asshole"

look.

"I'm touching myself," she said through gritted teeth.

"Where?"

"Where do you think?"

He slowed the car.

Getting the message, she replied, "I'm touching my clit."

"With what?"

She rolled her eyes.

"I'm touching myself with my fingers. Satisfied?"

"Which fingers?"

"Pointer and middle finger. Mostly the pointer finger."

"And what is it mostly doing?"

"I'm rubbing it up and down my clit."

His imagination gave him a nice visual of what she described. "How does it feel?"

"Awkward."

"I don't think your clit has emotion. How does it feel physically?"

"It feels like it's being stroked by a finger."

"How did it feel this morning?"

She didn't answer right away.

"It felt good, didn't it?" he prodded. "I want you to feel that again. Your body wants it. You want it. You deserve to feel good."

His words had lulled her eyes closed, and her body slouched in the seat. He could see her hand moving inside her shorts. Unlike her unzipped shorts, the crotch of his pants pressed tightly against him.

"What do you imagine when you masturbate alone at home?"

"Different things."

"Describe one."

"I once fantasized about getting it on with two NBA players."

"Yeah? And?"

"I'm sandwiched between them and they're both feeling me up. Their hands are all over my body."

"Are they gentle or rough?"

"Sometimes gentle, sometimes rough."

"Which way do you like it?"

"Both ways."

"If you had to pick one, which would it be?"

"I don't know. Depends on my mood."

"Pick one right now."

"...Rough."

His cock felt hard as steel. Abruptly, he pulled the car off the road. "Get out."

"The masturbating was working..."

He hopped out of the car and strode over

to the passenger side. Just as she got out, he pinned her to the side of the car. He hadn't touched her for several hours, and those hours had felt like a drought. Pulling her wrists above her head, he felt her breasts rise beneath him. He pressed himself farther into her, molding his body to her soft curves. When she looked up at him, startled, her eyes still glimmering from lust, he grew so turned on, he could have crushed her to the car. Pinning her wrists to the car with one hand, he thrust his other hand up her top.

"These basketball players, do they feel you up like this?" he asked, his hand firmly upon the rib cage.

Her breath seemed stuck in her throat. He moved his hand to a breast. Damn athletic bra. He palmed the tit as best he could through the tight garment. Her breath came out ragged.

"People can see us," she hissed.

They hadn't passed a car for several minutes, but even if the road wasn't presently deserted, he wouldn't care. He insinuated his fingers underneath the band of her bra and groped her.

"Are they this rough?"

She didn't answer. He dug his fingers into

her pliant flesh.

"Or rougher?"

He thrust the band of the bra over the top of the breast, giving him better access. She groaned when he began to maul her and gasped when he tugged the nipple.

"Even rougher?"

When he pinched her nipple, she yelped, "No!"

She had buttoned her shorts before getting out of the car, and he easily yanked them open. Like a child tearing into presents on Christmas morning, he thrust his hand into her shorts. The scent of her arousal, the feel of her wetness, made his head swim with desire. She moaned when he began stroking her.

"Are they rough down here, too?"

He fondled her gently as he awaited her answer.

"I don't know."

He rubbed her harder, rougher. Her lashes fluttered, and she began to squirm. All this writhing was going to undo him. He had a condom, but it was in the car, and he hadn't planned on using it until she was good and ready. But she was too hot right now not to fuck.

"We shouldn't…" she tried to protest.

"Which is precisely why we will."

Slowly, he inserted one, then two fingers into her snatch. Fuck. She was a furnace. She tried to break away but there was nowhere for her to go. He had her trapped and impaled.

"I'm serious," she said.

"No you're not," he whispered into her ear. "You didn't have a problem masturbating on the boat in front of the others."

"That was different. This is public."

"So what? So a car drives by. They see us for a few seconds. Maybe they know what we're up to, maybe they don't. They're just faceless strangers."

"What if they decide to pull over?"

His fingers searched the sweet spot within. "And if they did? Are you worried about giving them a show?"

He heard her swallow.

"Would you like that?"

"Hell no."

Her earlier struggles had waned, but she started anew until he found the spot he was looking for, the one that made her shiver and her eyes roll toward the back of her head.

"Let's say a car of mountain bikers drives

up," he told her. "Maybe they'll pull over to get a better look. Maybe they decide to get out of their car. Now they're not just faceless strangers, and they can see exactly what we're up to. The way you're groaning and whimpering is gonna make them hard. Would you like them to pull out their cocks and masturbate to the sight of you getting off against the car?"

She couldn't look him in the eye. A part of her was still resisting, but he detected the slight jerks of her body as he curled his fingers against her G-spot. If the fantasy he described to her were to come true, he wondered if he would limit himself to getting her off. He'd want to whip her around and fuck her from behind. Hard and rough.

However, the vehicle he saw approaching wasn't going to carry mountain bikers. Blue and red flashed in the corner of his eye. It was a cop.

CHAPTER FOUR

Ben gently disengaged from her and released her wrists. For a moment, Kimani was confused in mind and body. What did he intend? Was he going to leave her hanging on purpose? Or was he stepping back to unzip his jeans?

But then she heard the sirens.

Shit! As quickly as she could in her agitated state, she pulled her bra down and buttoned up her shorts. It was bad enough her shorts were wet from arousal, but now she had to face a cop, who may or may not bust them for public obscenity.

"Step away from the vehicle," the CHP officer said through his mic.

After they had complied, he emerged from his car. He was older and had himself a beer gut. With a frown, he looked them over. Kimani realized he had seen them outside the Jeep. Whether or not he knew what they were doing remained to be seen.

"License," the officer pronounced.

Ben took out his money clip and removed his license.

The cop took note of the Ben Franklins. "You rob a bank there?"

The tone wasn't lighthearted, and Ben gave him a sharp look.

"I don't have my license on me," Kimani said.

"I was the one driving," Ben said.

The cop gave Ben a hard stare, as if he wasn't sure Ben was telling the truth. He glanced between the license that was handed to him and Ben. "You here legally?"

Ben narrowed his eyes. "What's that supposed to mean?"

"ICE is cracking down on California," the cop replied. "They're not happy about the ones that got away down in the Bay Area."

She saw Ben's features harden.

"And because I'm Asian, you assume I'm here illegally?"

"Just saying, you don't look and sound like folks around here."

"Even if I *was* illegal, California's a sanctuary state. You're not supposed to cooperate with ICE without just cause."

The cop took a step toward Ben, his chest

out. "You telling me how to do my job?"

Seeing that Ben wasn't going to back down, Kimani jumped in. "Officer, it was so nice of you to stop and check that everything was okay with us."

He turned his frown to her and looked her up and down. Ben seemed to notice him leering, and stiffened. She put her hand on Ben's arm before he said anything. "We appreciate it, sir."

The officer looked at Ben again. "Wait here. And don't move."

"Tosser," Ben murmured as he glared at the cop's back.

"It's not worth it," she said. "You went to Howard. You know that in his eyes, you're guilty just because your skin's the 'wrong' color."

"Doesn't mean we can't call him on his shit."

"Yeah, but you think that's going to stop him from being a racist? He's just gonna find some reason to throw you in jail for a while. Just to mess with you. Because he can."

"He can learn he shouldn't. Jail doesn't scare me. It wouldn't be the first time I've had to sit behind bars."

"In America? Bad shit happens in our

jails."

He gave her a searching look. "You worried about me?"

"You haven't done anything wrong, and I wouldn't want anything to happen to innocent people. Besides, I still need to pee."

His shoulders relaxed and his expression softened.

"Look," she said, "if you want to take him on, I've got your back. I'll sit in jail with you. I've got as much beef as you, right?"

"More."

"I just don't want a jerk ruining our time."

Ben said nothing as the cop walked back to them. "This isn't a parking spot. I could give you a ticket—"

She could see Ben was ready to retort with something like, "Then why don't you?"

"—but I'll let you off with a warning," the cop finished, handing Ben back his license.

Kimani breathed a sigh of relief when Ben took the license and said nothing. To the cop, she said, "Thank you, sir."

Ben opened the car door for her, and she climbed in. She watched in the side-view mirror as Ben came up to the cop on his way around the car. *Just get in the car*, she pleaded silently. He stopped in front of the officer. Ben was almost a foot taller and in much better shape, but a cop was a cop. The officer puffed out his chest.

"Hey, bae, we gotta get back so I can make dinner," she called to him.

Ben glanced in her direction, then back at the officer. Without a word, he continued around the car and got into the driver's seat. The cop shook his head and strode back to his vehicle. Ben started the car and pulled back onto the highway. The officer followed until they turned off the highway onto the road that would take them to the cabin. Kimani didn't relax until she saw the CHP's car continue on the highway.

"You've got a lot of forbearance," Ben commented.

"In a good way or bad?"

"It's neither good, nor bad. But it was the smart thing to do, not to waste more time with that prat."

Leaning the side of her head against her hand, she blew out a long breath. "I don't know. Like you said, someone's got to call him out on crap like that, but you never know who you're dealing with. I remember when my father got pulled over for nothing more than a DWB, and I was scared to death that something would happen to him. These days, standing up for yourself can get you killed. But if you don't stand up, are you being complicit? A coward?"

"Every situation's different."

She looked out the window, feeling unsettled. She didn't like that she had to make nice with a man who didn't deserve it. It felt like he had gotten away with something he shouldn't have. But she had been fairly certain by the cop's demeanor that he would have made trouble for them if they'd made any waves.

Ben's voice cut into her thoughts. "Like you said, it's not worth it."

"You really think so?"

"Would I rather sit in jail when I could be spending that time making your body quiver and shake? Hell no."

"Then why were you antagonizing the guy?"

"I wasn't in a good mood. He interrupted us."

Which was a good thing, she considered. She had let Ben mess with her enough.

"It was fun hearing you call me 'bae' though," he said, looking over at her.

She flushed. "It's just what came out first

because I was worried you were going to mess with the cop still."

He nodded as he focused back on the road. "I like it."

She cleared her throat. "So when and where were you behind bars?"

"In Hong Kong when I was a juvenile delinquent."

"What were you jailed for?"

"I was in a brawl at a *dai pai dong*—it's kind of like an open-air food market."

"Do you miss being in Hong Kong? Or China?"

He glanced at her. "Are you just making conversation?"

"What's wrong with making conversation?"

He didn't say anything. She couldn't figure him out. One instant he was offering up all kinds of information about himself, the next he somehow managed to steer the conversation from answering her questions.

"You still need to piss?" he asked.

"Ugh. Now that you mention it…"

"Take your shorts off."

"That's okay. What if we get pulled over again?"

"You think there's more than one patrol

officer out here?"

"You never know."

"Just undo them."

"I'd rather not."

He raised a brow. "Why?"

"I'm not in the mood anymore."

"Doesn't matter. You will be."

She bristled. This is what came of giving in to the man in the first place. Now he felt he could exploit her lust anytime and anywhere. "I just want to get to the cabin."

"The sooner you comply, the sooner we'll get there."

Did that mean he would pull the car over if she didn't do what he said? Probably. How much longer before they reached the cabin? Could she hold it?

"The cabin's still fifteen minutes away," he informed her.

She groaned. "Just pull over so I can do my business behind a bush."

"If I pull over, I get to pick up where we left off after you go."

Her mouth fell open. She didn't like either of her options, but which one was worse?

CHAPTER FIVE

She looked away quickly, but Ben saw the flare in her eyes. The way her lips pursed in obvious displeasure was almost adorable. It didn't bother him that she was feisty; he liked her, attitude and all. But he didn't quite understand why she was resisting. Dealing with the cop had soured her mood, but this wasn't the first time she'd held back.

He gave her a few minutes to weigh her options. He could tell she was trying to come up with a third alternative, a way out.

When it was clear she hadn't come up with anything, she asked, "Are those my only choices?"

"You want to opt for what's behind curtain number three?"

"What's behind curtain number three?"

"It's a surprise."

"I always hated that game show," she grumbled after a moment of contemplation.

"You hate uncertainty."

47

"Who doesn't?"

"Sometimes it pays to take risks. You took a big one participating in the Scarlet Auction."

"Yeah, but if I don't like my situation, I can walk away."

"And give up the two thousand dollar deposit."

"Yeah, nifty how they set it up like that."

"You feel like walking away right now?"

She gave him a restrained glare. "How can I? I've got to pee."

"I'm giving you three ways to relieve yourself."

"Three?"

"If you think you can hold it all the way back to the cabin, you can use the bathroom there, but then you choose to submit to what's behind curtain number three."

"That's not a choice. How can I agree to something when I don't even know what it is?"

"Everything is a choice, pet. Even doing nothing is a choice you make."

She stiffened when he called her pet, which he deliberately did to test her. "So which is it going to be?" he pressed.

With a vexed sigh, she reached for the

button of her shorts.

Interesting. He would have thought pissing on the side of the road the easiest option, but maybe that was because he was a guy. Maybe pissing was a more delicate act for women.

Watching her, he wondered how far he could take her, how he could take down her resistance. If he had more than a week, or if Kimani proved more amenable, he might obliterate all of her sensibilities.

"Good choice," he said.

"I bet for you, they're all good choices," she retorted.

He smiled. "Yeah, they are, but my top pick would've been curtain number three. Now pull that zipper down nice and slow."

Taking in a breath, she drew the zipper down. Because she wasn't wearing any knickers, he would let her keep the shorts on. He shouldn't have let her buy underwear at the CVS, so he could be assured she would always go commando. But she did still have a lot of walls that needed knocking down, and he couldn't do it being an asshole a hundred percent of the time.

"My turn," he said when she was about to reach a hand into her shorts.

Grasping her thigh, he inched her closer to him before settling his hand at her crotch. It was a warm and inviting space. Her curls there were soft and delicate. She inhaled sharply when his fingers grazed lower. Still wet.

He wanted to adjust his jeans, but with a hand buried in her shorts, he needed the other one on the steering wheel. He alternated between looking at her face and the road ahead. Her brow furrowed as if she was concentrating on something. Not pissing her pants, maybe. Or maybe she was still resisting. But why would that be? She had let him masturbate her twice before already— once on the boat with the others in plain view, no less.

He was thinking too much. Sex, and even the seduction prior to sex, rarely required thinking on his part. Even with the ones who played hard-to-get, like the daughter of a Japanese tycoon who held old-fashioned notions that the Chinese were inferior to the people of the rising sun, he'd rarely had to deviate from his modus operandi. The challenge of seducing princesses like her didn't much interest him. And when it became clear he wasn't going to bother, her demeanor had changed and she began to seek out his attention. It hadn't taken long after that before he had her wriggling beneath him in bed, gasping and crying out in the high-pitched manner of female anime characters. It had grated on his ears, so they'd only fucked once.

But Kimani was different. She was a challenge that *did* interest him. He didn't know why. Sure, she was lush. A hot piece of ass. But in a modestly confident instead of in-your-face way. She was a little quick to judge and opinionated, but that shouldn't matter because he had bought her for sex, not to be his mate. He should stay focused on the sex.

He slid his fingers up and down her clit. Her breathing became erratic. Her lashes fluttered quickly, and she grasped the armrest with her right hand. When his digits circled the engorged nub, she surrendered a soft moan.

"Good. I want you to get nice and aroused for me."

The road curved a lot, but he managed to maneuver the steering wheel with one hand without losing the rhythm of his stroking. She closed her eyes. Muted grunts—little pleas for more—escaped from her throat.

She knit her brows. "Ohhh..."

He could feel her tighten below. What he wouldn't give to be buried in her right now as the regions of her sex clenched. She gripped the armrest harder. Eyes still closed, she moaned something unintelligible.

He dipped his fingers lower and passed over her pisshole. She nearly leaped out of her skin with a startled gasp.

"Did you know orgasms can be more intense on a full bladder?" he asked, noting that it hadn't taken her long to reach her current level of arousal.

She managed to shake her head a little.

"Want to see if it's true?"

She didn't reply, but her eyes flew open when he caressed her urethral opening again. Her mouth hung open, and she probably couldn't close it if she tried.

"Jesus," she pleaded.

"Does my pet want to come?"

Her left hand gripped the seat belt. She looked as if she were bracing for a steep descent off the top of a roller coast. He wanted to see her fall into pieces.

"Does she?" he asked.

"...un-hunh..." she whimpered.

"Ask to come."

"M-May I come?"

"Please."

"P-Please may I come?"

He returned his gaze to the window because he had just pulled up in front of the cabin. He pulled his hand out of her shorts. "You may. Later."

She looked confused. "Wha...?"

He shut off the engine, grabbed the keys, and opened his door. "Next time, do what I say, do it faster, and things will turn out better."

Her expression went from shock to anger. Her glare told him he was a bigger jerk than she had thought. He got out of the car and adjusted his crotch.

Learning the hard way wasn't fun, but it was more effective. And since they only had a week—correction, six days—he didn't have time to piss around with being too gentle and nurturing. He had gone over twenty-four hours in her company, seeing her naked, feeling her body, watching her come. It was finally going to be his turn.

CHAPTER SIX

When Ben opened the passenger-side door, Kimani didn't want to get out. She wanted to stay in the Jeep and have him finish what he'd been doing.

How could he be so nice one minute, buying her clothes and taking her to tea, and be such a jerk the next?

"Come on," he said, holding all the bags from their shopping excursion.

"I need a minute to compose myself," she responded through gritted teeth.

He gave a her a stern look. "What did I just say?"

She had a childish impulse to grab those fancy Louis Vuitton shades off his face and crumple them to pieces. With a huff, she zipped and buttoned her shorts, then got out of the car.

I did not sign up for this.

Yes, you did.

She shook her head at the devil's advocate inside of her. Right now she was too upset for rational thought. Her body still vibrated from arousal, still craved the promise of a more intense orgasm. Based on how quickly the tension had mounted inside her and how his caress had sent waves of pleasure throughout her, she had expected his statement about a full bladder to prove true for her.

But now she wouldn't get to find out.

He nodded toward the cabin, indicating she should go first, almost as if he intended to be chivalrous. But he was far from chivalrous, making her walk into the cabin to face all the others in her current state.

"Don't you need to use the bathroom?" he asked when she didn't move.

She searched for his eyes behind his shades and found them. "Fuck you."

He looked amused. For a second. The next, his hand was curled around the back of her neck, pulling her head toward him. The jerk had moves as swift as Jet Li.

"That's going to cost you, pet."

After he released her, she stumbled in her attempt to walk forward but straightened when he grabbed her to steady her.

"I'm fine," she snapped, not wanting him to touch her. Bad things happened when he touched her.

He let her go, and she stomped to the cabin door. Vince opened on the second ring of the doorbell. The others were in the great room, the men lounging on the sofa, their feet propped on human footstools. Lisa, Claire and Ryan were still in their birthday suits. Kimani wondered how long they had been made to kneel on all fours.

"About time," Jake drawled. He had been the one that all the women wanted at the auction, but Kimani could only see him now as ugly. "Did you forget Slut #2 is supposed to make dinner?"

"Where were you?" Jason asked Ben.

A golf tournament was playing on the television screen, which came down from an in-ceiling motorized lift mount.

"Shopping," Ben replied.

Claire perked up.

Jake rolled his eyes. "Pussy stuff."

"Can your girl make dinner fast?" Jason asked. "I'm starving."

"I've got to use the bathroom first," Kimani answered, but before she moved, she turned to Ben. "May I, sir?"

"You may," he said, his tone no longer stern.

Taking the bag that held her purchases, she hurried to the bathroom. Her body was still tense down there, so the pee didn't come out right away. Relieving herself had never felt so unsatisfying. She cursed Ben as she sat on the toilet. She did not enjoy having to ask his permission to use the bathroom but didn't want to risk his teaching her another "lesson." As if a man in his position didn't already get anything he wanted, however he wanted, he had to lord over her body functions, too?

I'm just role-playing, she reminded herself. *This is for the* Tribune*, your career.*

The longer she hung around, the more she could witness. She needed to deepen the rapport between her and the other women if she hoped to include their stories.

Feeling a little better, she washed up before heading to the kitchen, glad to be making dinner instead of posing as furniture. She noticed Ben wasn't around as she searched for something fast and easy. Finding pasta, she pulled out a pot to boil water. Opening the fridge, she looked for ingredients to make a salad. Chopping the vegetables also made her feel better and allowed the last of the agitation in her body to simmer down.

Ben wasn't gone long, but he let her have her space, choosing instead to work on his iPad at the dining table. Jake, after helping himself to a shot of whiskey, sauntered over to Ben.

"Your chick must've done something nice to earn clothes," Jake said. "She suck you off good?"

"What's it to you?" Ben asked without looking up from his tablet.

"Well, I have certain rules and expectations I like to enforce here at the cabin, and it helps when we're all on the same page."

"Like what?"

"You take your slut shopping, all the other sluts are going to want to go shopping, too. And I don't do that kind of shit."

"So don't."

Jake pressed his lips together. "I just don't want them getting the wrong idea."

"I don't see your girl pushing for anything against your wishes."

"Yeah, I put my foot down in no uncertain terms on day one. You've only got one chance at making a first impression." When Ben didn't respond, Jake continued. "It's not just in play, you know. Women in general, whether they're into BDSM or not, don't want to be treated too well. The more you treat them like shit, the more they want you. Just like they want a guy who sleeps around. It's why nice guys always finish last."

Ben looked at Jake. "Are you giving me this advice because you're worried I'm nice?"

He's not that nice, Kimani wanted to inform Jake as she dumped sliced red onions into the salad bowl.

Jake looked over in her direction. "Anytime you think your slut needs to learn who's boss, just send her my way."

Ben's jaw immediately tightened, but an incoming call to his cell cut off his response. He glanced to see who it was before accepting the call, walking away from the table toward the hall.

Kimani wouldn't have cared where Ben went except for the fact that Jake had wandered into the kitchen.

"You look better without clothes," he said after perusing her from head to toe. "You should've stuck with me. I know how to handle women like you."

She bit her tongue to keep from retorting that it had been his decision to sell her.

Instead, she kept her gaze on the cucumber she was slicing.

"That's all I was doing that first day," Jake said, "establishing our roles: mine as the head of the house. You as the sexual servants I bought. You get to live out your little fantasies being dominated by men. That Chinaman can't fulfill your fantasies."

She glanced up sharply at him. "Does Ben know you use words like that? I don't think he'd appreciate being called that."

"What are you, some politically correct bitch?" He leaned in close enough for her to smell the whiskey on his breath. "I bet I could fuck the political correctness out of you nice and good."

Deciding she'd rather stand next to a leper, she stepped back and reached for the bottles of olive oil and balsamic vinegar to make a dressing. Jake leaned against the counter and observed her with a look that was half interest, half disgust.

"Maybe I should buy you back," he mused aloud. "Give you a proper pounding."

The prospect made her skin crawl. Ben wouldn't let that happen. Right?

"I'm not a good slut," she muttered.

"That's 'cause Ben's a wuss."

Standing in the corner, she had no room to maneuver when he bridged the short distance between them. "You ever had white cock?"

No, and I certainly don't want yours.

He leered at her. "You're on the lighter side. Somewhere your ancestors took white cock."

"Not willingly," she retorted.

"You don't know that. Who knows? Maybe once you go white, you don't go back to black. So how about it? Let Ching Chong know you want dick from a real man."

He brushed the knuckles of his right hand along her right arm. She flinched away. "Get your stinking KKK hands off me."

The area about his mouth went white. Her arms went up as she braced herself to be hit. But the sound of Ben's voice stayed Jake from whatever he was about to do.

"Call me tomorrow, then," Ben was saying into his cell, his voice growing louder as he neared the kitchen.

Jake narrowed his eyes at her. "Changed my mind. Your cunt's not worth it."

With a final glare, he turned around and nearly walked into Ben.

"You're not messing with my purchase,

are you?" Ben asked with a frown.

"Not a chance," Jake replied. "I couldn't be happier you took her off my hands."

"Good. I don't touch yours. You don't touch mine."

"Yeah, yeah," Jake grumbled as he exited the kitchen.

Kimani went back to making the salad, spilling the vinegar on the counter when she tipped the bottle too quickly. Her quickened heartbeat hadn't gone back to normal yet. For a moment, she had been sure she was going to end up with a second bruise to go with her first.

"What was Jake doing in the kitchen?" Ben asked, watching her.

"Being Jake," she muttered.

"He give you trouble?"

She considered telling him the truth. She would like nothing more than to see Ben, if he were so inclined, beat the crap out of Jake. But what if Jake threw them out of his cabin? Without having exchanged numbers with the women, she'd have no way of contacting them. And she couldn't leave Claire. It was fortunate that Jake had ended up with someone whose disposition tolerated his assholeness.

"Nothing I can't handle."

Her response, however, felt like a lie. She couldn't have been more relieved to hear Ben's voice. And it sucked. She didn't want to have to depend on Ben, whom she wondered whether she could trust a hundred percent, given that they'd known each other all of thirty hours. But if Ben hadn't arrived, she'd be stuck with Jake. The thought made her shudder.

That was what was so messed up with the setup of the Scarlet Auction. The women were put in powerless situations—and not just for the sake of kinky role-playing.

As she tossed the salad, she silently vowed that she would write the story that would put an end to the Scarlet Auction.

CHAPTER SEVEN

"**D**ude, how many calls you going to get in one evening?" Derek asked over the table when Ben's phone rang for the third time during dinner.

"It's Monday morning in Hong Kong," Ben explained as he got up. He almost didn't want to let Jake and Kimani out of his sight. She had been agitated in the kitchen. But since she was having her spaghetti and salad over with the other women at the coffee table, she was probably okay.

He took the call out on the back patio. It was May, the second eldest of his three sisters.

"I need you to talk to Father about the bodyguard," she said in Cantonese, her dialect of choice when she was upset. "I'm sick and tired of it. *You* don't have one all the time."

May was a sharp woman, so the response to such a statement should have been obvious to her.

"The fact that I don't always have Bataar with me has no persuasion value," he stated. "Remember, Father tried to stick a bodyguard on me, too."

Ben had ditched his bodyguard enough times that his father had finally stopped keeping track. Ben liked Bataar, though, and kept the man on payroll. May had done her fair share of eluding her bodyguard, but their father wasn't going to give up as easily for a daughter, especially after the recent high-profile kidnappings that included a young fashion heiress.

"And I'm six-two, a hundred and ninety pounds with advanced training in kung fu," he added.

"The bodyguard makes Little Red nervous," she said of her girlfriend. "She can't be herself. She wouldn't stay the night at my place."

"You're trying to convince the wrong person. First of all, if Red wants to be with you bad enough, she'll find a way to deal with it. Secondly, *I* would pay for your bodyguard if Father didn't."

"Some help you are! I don't know why I even bothered to call you."

Ben knew she had called because he was the closest ally she had. Growing up, she and Ben would sometimes team up against their older sister, Phyllis, who was in line to be the company's CFO and prone to lecturing them on how they should behave. As kids, if Ben was confined to his room as punishment, May would sneak him comics under the door. And May butted heads with their father almost as often as Ben had before he'd turned things around.

"I'll talk to your bodyguard," he offered. "Maybe there are some things he can do differently so you won't feel his presence so much."

"I guess that's better than nothing," she huffed.

Her partial mollification indicated to Ben that this wasn't the last he was going to hear about the bodyguard. Glancing into the cabin through the patio doors, Ben saw that Jake was no longer at the dining table.

"May, I've got to go."

"Talk to the bodyguard soon. Now would be good."

"I'll call in the morning—evening for you."

"Why can't you do it now?"

"I have to check on something."

"On what?"

He wasn't about to explain to his younger sister that he needed to check on a woman he had bought for two hundred thousand US dollars.

"Nothing of concern to you," he replied.

She sniffed out part of the truth anyway. "Hmm, like a woman?"

"Goodbye, May."

"Is she someone you're just banging—"

But he had hung up and walked back inside. Jake was at the bar, making himself a vodka tonic. Ben glanced over at where the women sat around the coffee table.

Kimani was cleaning spaghetti off herself. It looked like the whole pasta bowl had landed on her lap. Her legs were covered in sauce.

"Sir, may I get some towels for her?" Claire, a young and slender blond, asked Jake.

"Sure, because you've been a good little slut today," Jake replied, "and I'm such a nice guy."

Kimani gave him a hard look. Ben wondered if Jake had anything to do with the spilled spaghetti.

"You can use the bathroom in my room to

wash up," Ben told her.

"Maybe one of the other chicks can lick her clean."

Not in the mood to indulge Jake, he looked at Kimani. "Go on."

Claire came back with paper towels, and she and Lisa helped clean the mess on the table so that Kimani could go wash up. Even pasta sauce looked good on her. Ben thought about following Kimani upstairs to clean her himself. Instead, he went over to Jake.

"How did spaghetti end up all over her?" Ben asked.

"Want one?" Jake replied after taking a swig of his drink.

"No." Ben didn't drink much and had even less desire than usual in present company.

"Her bowl was right on the edge of the table. I accidentally bumped it when I walked by." Jake turned to Claire. "Isn't that right, slut?"

Claire nodded her head vigorously.

"Hey, cuz!" Jason called. "Jake's going to help me become a sports agent."

Ben turned to his cousin. "I was going to talk to Father about having you work on the resort in Thailand with me."

"Yeah, but the family doesn't really need

me on that when they've got you. Besides, sports is much more interesting than real estate development. Maybe I can work on recruiting Tyrell Jenkins and take that off your hands."

Jenkins was the prospect that Ben hoped would sign with the Golden Phoenix, one of the teams currently struggling in the Chinese Basketball Association.

Ben glanced at Jake. "Your idea?"

"I think Jason would be great at it," Jake answered.

Bullshit. Jason had zero professional negotiating experience, and while he was an exuberant fan, he knew little of sports management. Jake would walk all over him.

Now, it was possible that Jake was acting out of friendship. He and Jason had been close since they were dormmates in college, but Ben wasn't going to give Jake the benefit of the doubt so easily.

"Let him do it," Jake urged. "It's not like being a sports agent is your real job."

But Ben's father, the head of the Lee Family Corporation, was the Golden Phoenix's biggest fan and patron. He wouldn't want just anyone taking the lead. The coach and team manager had allowed the

Lee family to intervene because the last sports agent had burned them, wasting time with subpar talent while asking for large contracts.

"You've never expressed an interest in the business of sports before," Ben said to Jason.

Jason shrugged. "I've always liked basketball."

Since Ben was the only son, Jason was the closest thing to a brother to him. He wanted to support his cousin, and for the first time, Ben realized how frustrated his own father must have felt, seeing a family member who wasn't living up to his potential.

"All right, let's talk about it later," Ben said. He wasn't going to discuss the matter with Jake around.

Taking up his pasta bowl, Ben reheated the food in the microwave. Several texts chimed on his phone.

"Dude, you need to learn how to take a vacation," Derek said.

Ben scanned the messages to see that none were urgent.

"Did you know that none of the women have their cellphones?" Ben asked the other guys. "The Scarlet Auction took them."

"So? Sluts don't need cellphones," Jake

said.

"Yeah," Derek seconded, "phones would just be a distraction."

"It's to protect the privacy of the bidders."

"What about the privacy of the women?" Ben inquired.

"Given who we are, we're more likely to be the victims of blackmail and shit like that."

"A lot of the bidders are married men," Derek added, "though if I ever get married, it's gonna be an open marriage, know what I mean?"

The microwave finished just as Ben reached his tolerance level for conversation with overgrown frat boys. He took the bowl out of the microwave and headed upstairs to see how Kimani was doing.

Another text came in as he climbed the stairs. It was from Stephens, his special projects manager based in the US. It read:

Got the info you wanted.

CHAPTER EIGHT

S ince the items they had bought in town were in his room, Kimani decided to take a shower. She'd had one yesterday but didn't have the conditioner she needed. Conditioning was important given that she had styled her hair to appeal to as much of the audience of bidders as possible at the Scarlet Auction. If she had hair like Lisa's, she could probably go days without washing or conditioning.

The shower felt great, a steamy oasis from the testosterone that ran the place. When she emerged and wrapped a towel around herself, she felt rejuvenated and focused on her task at hand. She was going to get the story that would land her a job at the *Tribune*. She wasn't going to let a jerk like Jake get in the way.

Ben, however, was a different story. He got in the way—in a big way. She shouldn't be letting him distract her. How could she be so easily seduced by him? And here she thought she was different from the other women. While it was true that she didn't have Claire's romantic fancies of falling in love during her week as a sex toy, she should have been able to resist Ben's seduction.

And don't forget you're mad at him for leaving you high and dry—correction, high and wet.

Recalling how his fingers had felt against her, how his digits probed places that sent currents zinging up her spine, warmed her as much as the steam in the bathroom. She should never have let him touch her in the first place. She had known that doing so was stumbling off a cliff.

But he had felt so good. And it wasn't just how he caressed her. When she had lain against him on the patio chair last night, his body had provided a warm security that comforted as much as it titillated.

That was it. She was grateful to Ben. Finding herself in a high-stress situation, stuck in the boondocks of Northern California, and worried for her welfare after Jake had struck her across the cheek, she saw Ben as her protector. Yesterday, he had lent her clothes, saw that she had lunch, and allowed her to nap in his bed.

But he had his asshole moments. He wasn't a pure knight in shining armor. He had bought her for sex, after all.

She wiped the condensation off the bathroom mirror and looked at herself. How far was she willing to go for her story? She didn't have a problem going undercover, but she hadn't planned on having sex. She had planned to test the man who won her to see what would happen if she said no to something or decided she wanted to back out of the arrangement altogether. She may have consented to participate in the Scarlet Auction, but a woman had a right to change her mind.

However, she already knew the Auction had set things up so it was unlikely a woman would back out. There were the imposing contracts and nondisclosure agreements signed before multiple attorneys, the nonrefundable application fee of two thousand dollars, and the fact that a woman who didn't complete the entire week to the satisfaction of the purchaser would not receive a penny.

So far Ben hadn't pushed himself onto her, but a man could only be so patient. She sensed he had gone easy on her their first day together, but he was making his expectations known.

It was bad enough she had compromised the story by becoming sexually involved with one of the subjects, but she was determined to get the best story that she could and let Sam, the editor of the *Tribune*, sort it out.

Best not to make things more complicated, however, between herself and Ben. Tonight, she would focus on the other women. They hadn't had much of a chance to talk during dinner because they didn't know if they were allowed to. She had asked Claire, in a whisper, how she was doing. The young blond had smiled in return. Kimani hoped that meant Jake hadn't hit her. Lisa, a very slender woman with long black hair, and Ryan, a lithe redhead and perhaps the most confident of the women, seemed in good spirits.

The women slept downstairs in what looked and felt like a basement dungeon, but the upside was that, away from the men, they could talk freely. While on the boat this morning, Kimani and Ryan, Derek's purchase, had gotten into an interesting conversation, and Kimani had not yet had the chance to write down notes.

And she still had to call Sam and give him an update and assure him that she was still safe. For that, she would need to use Ben's cellphone again, as she had done yesterday.

He was there when she stepped out of the bathroom and into the bedroom. How was it he could look so sexy just leaning against the dresser? The plastic bag with the clothes from the thrift store lay next to his hip. *Damn.* She should have brought the clothes with her into the bathroom to change into. Now she stood with only a towel around her. At least it was on the larger side. Still, she could use as many layers of protection as possible. He didn't leer or ogle, but he took in all of her.

"Thought you might want to finish dinner," he said, indicating a bowl of pasta next to him.

She remembered dishing out all the pasta. "Isn't that yours?"

"It's yours now."

She couldn't imagine a guy his size not eating. "Don't you want it? Or do you not like it?"

"The pasta tasted fine, but I don't need to eat."

She gave him a funny look.

"I often have just one meal a day," he said.

"'Cause you're too busy to eat?"

"Because I choose to."

"Why?"

"It's a health choice. Anyway, the pasta is yours if you want it."

He held out the bowl and a fork. She was still hungry, but should she change first? She didn't want to reach over and get too close to him. She checked to make sure her towel was secure before accepting the fork and bowl. She sat down in a chair a comfortable distance from him.

"Are you sure you don't want to have some?" she asked. "I had salad, so there's no way I could finish all this."

"Just eat what you can."

While she ate, he scrolled through his phone.

"Is this a working vacation for you?" she inquired.

"Sort of."

He seemed to be reading something.

"Something the matter?"

He looked up from his phone in surprise. "Why do you ask that?"

"You just looked a little unhappy."

"How could you tell?"

She wasn't sure. The guy was not expressive, but her senses had been on high alert most of her time here. "I don't know. Just picked up on it somehow. Is everything okay?"

She wasn't sure why she cared.

"I was reading an update to the EIR for a property we're interested in developing."

"An Environmental Impact Report?"

He nodded. "Remediation is required."

"Where is the property?"

"Oakland."

She perked up. "You do a lot of business in Oakland?" she asked as she pushed the pasta around the bowl.

"What do you consider a lot?"

"Have you developed property in the city before?"

"We've funded a number of developments. You're interested in real estate?"

"I'm interested in Oakland. I was born there. Went to a preschool in Chinatown. Was one of two black kids in the class."

"Did you live in Chinatown?"

"No, but it was the most affordable preschool in town. Childcare is a big issue in the upcoming mayoral race." Since Ben hadn't told her about his uncle, she couldn't ask him directly about it. She thought for a moment before saying, "One of the candidates shares your last name."

He was staring at her rather intently. "He's my uncle."

Kimani pretended to be surprised. "On your dad's side?"

"The youngest of five sons. He immigrated to the United States when he was fourteen."

"Are you expected to help with the campaign?"

"I do what I can."

"Do you walk precincts or—let me guess—fundraise."

"There's only so much I can do." He looked down at his phone. "It's for you."

He held the phone up for her to see the text. It was from Sam and contained only two words:

Call me.

He was probably worried about her. She reached for the phone. "Can I use your cell again?"

But Ben withdrew it. "You want the phone? You've got to find out what's behind curtain number three."

CHAPTER NINE

Even in a frown, her lips looked luscious. He wanted to take them. Smother them. Devour them.

He had lucked out on timing, though catching her in the shower would have been better. He had thought about walking in on her but had refrained, knowing he would impose himself on her later. She looked too hot in that towel for him to do nothing. She had the perfect body, fit and still athletic but, as she no longer kept up the same level of training as she had when she was playing ball, softened in all the right places.

Given her reticence, he had been patient with her. He had never had to wait for sex before—and he had *paid* for it this time. With a woman who wanted the money badly enough that she was willing to trade her body. He knew she hadn't signed up for the Scarlet Auction for fun or she would have welcomed his advances more than she had.

However, he'd see to it that by the end, money would be a secondary consideration for her.

"What's behind curtain number three?" she asked.

"I told you before...it's a surprise," he replied.

"That's not fair. How am I supposed to make an informed decision?"

"Who says life is fair?"

Her nostrils flared.

"I'll give you a safety word. You don't like anything, just say the word 'mercy.'"

That relaxed her. A little.

"Is there a reason you're not telling me?" she tried.

"Is there a reason you need to know?"

Answering with a question clearly irritated her. She retorted, "I asked first."

He crossed his arms. "You want to know why? Because *not* knowing amps up the anticipation."

With a swallow, she looked away. If his answer rattled her, it was her own fault for asking.

"What's your need to know?"

She met his challenging gaze. "I want to know what I'm getting into. Like you said before, I don't like uncertainty."

"Did you know what you were getting into when you signed up for the Scarlet Auction?"

"I imagined the worst."

He cocked his head to one side, finding her response strange. "Only the worst?"

She seemed to regret what she said. "I mean...I had heard stories that didn't turn out so well. Some guys can be real jerks, you know."

"But you needed the money badly enough that you were willing to risk it and have sex with a jerk."

"Something like that."

"If that's what you're committed to, why are you so worried about what's behind curtain number three?"

"What if you're into some kink that I'm not into?"

"Jake said you told the Scarlet Auction questionnaire that you were up for anything."

"I guess—but with the right guy."

"I'm the right guy."

Her lower lip fell, and it was all he could do not to bridge the distance between them, yank the towel off her, and take those lips. Lips that he had paid two hundred thousand dollars for.

He did push off the dresser, and she

immediately tensed as if bracing for fight or flight.

"So what's it going to be?"

She looked at his cell, which he had placed on the dresser.

"You're going to honor the safety word, right?" she asked when she returned her gaze to his, her eyes piercing into him. "It said in the legal contract that everything has to be mutually agreed upon first."

She had spoken quickly, as if she didn't believe her own assertion.

He held her stare. "I didn't sign any contracts."

Her face fell, but she gathered herself. "But one could argue that the terms of the contract apply to extensions of the original arrangement."

He wasn't a lawyer, but it seemed like she was grasping at straws. "You can sue Jake for breach of contract. And you could sue me, too, just for the hell of it, but how does that help you in the here and now?"

Her eyes steeled against him. She was a smart woman. She knew, even if her claim about extending the terms of the contract to third parties held any water, that (a) he wasn't afraid of lawsuits; (b) she didn't have the resources to go after him; and (c) the real damage would have been done long before any lawsuit could occur.

She wasn't happy with the situation. Consequently, she wasn't happy with him. He got to run the show, and she didn't like that. Probably resented him for it. He could see her searching her mind for a card to play, but all the high cards were in his hand. She saw that, but she wasn't ready to give up just yet.

"Are you suggesting you're not going to honor your safety word?"

"I wouldn't have provided you one if I wasn't. Now, how badly do you need to talk to Sam?"

She huffed. "Can I have a minute to think about it?"

"Sure. But the towel comes off while you think."

Her anger flared twofold. She was probably cursing him in her head right now. It didn't bother him that she did. It intrigued him. While it was messed up that the Scarlet Auction had taken her cellphone, he wasn't a nice enough guy not to use that to his advantage. Especially since she had lied about who Sam was, telling him some bullshit about Sam formerly being a man but was now a female friend, one who worried about her.

Stephens, who handled special projects for him in the States, had found out that Samuel Green was the editor of the *San Francisco Tribune* and married with two kids.

"I haven't had a chance to do anything for you yet," she said, rising to her feet.

His cock perked. "Such as?"

She took a step toward him. "How about I get the cellphone if I suck you off?"

Fuck. It was a tempting offer, but was she really hoping to do that? He had thought about sliding his cock into that hot mouth of hers multiple times.

"You want to give me a blow job?" he tested.

"Don't I get to touch you?"

His whole body tensed, screaming for the prospect. She took another step forward, doing her best to look and sound sultry. She didn't have to play the seductress, however. He had been willing to fuck her the day he saw her.

"I assume you've had a blow job before?" she inquired.

He laughed. Over a hundred easily. "You any good?"

"Sure. At least, I've never failed to get a guy off. You're not...shy...are you?"

Was she challenging him? He decided to press back. "So you'd rather suck my cock than see what's behind curtain number three?"

"I thought, since you've already gotten me to come, it was your turn."

He smirked. "How do you know curtain number three doesn't already involve deepthroating?"

At that, her little attempt to seduce him faltered. Most guys would probably have taken the blow job by now, but what he had in mind was so much better than a quick crotch sneeze.

"It's curtain number three or nothing, pet. But don't worry. You'll still have the chance to blow me."

She seethed for a few seconds before lifting her chin. "I'll agree to curtain number three if there's no penetration."

She was trying to dictate the terms? He assessed her stubbornly set jaw. As much as he disliked Jake, he had to agree that setting the expectations correctly at the beginning mattered.

He could see *himself* being a total jerk and

making penetration a requisite for getting the cellphone, but he was intrigued by the challenge. Could he go without burying his cock in her?

His body objected, his cock stretching the confines of his pants in protest. But, for now, his mind still held control. He had to prove to himself that he didn't want her that badly, no matter how blue his balls got.

A corner of his mouth curled. "No penetration. Just know, however, that when you beg for it, you won't get it. Because that's what we agreed to."

She scrunched her face, indicating she doubted he could be that serious. He was fucking serious. If he had to suffer, she would, too.

"Fine," she said.

"Fine, what?"

"Fine, I'll go with curtain number three."

I made my choice, but I don't like it, said her eyes and tone.

He returned a small smile. *Doesn't matter. You will.*

"What's the safety word again?" she demanded, but her breath faintly quivered.

"Mercy."

Anticipation swelled in his groin. It was

bloody time to have some real fun.

"I get the phone as soon as we're done?" she asked.

"As soon as you've completed everything behind curtain number three."

"You didn't specify that before."

"You think I'm going to be okay if, five minutes in, you use your safety word?"

"What if I'm not able to *complete* everything?"

"You will."

"What if I use my safety word twenty minutes in? How long does curtain number three last?"

"If you use your safety word before we're done, then you haven't completed curtain number three. As for how long it lasts, that's up to you and how well you're participating."

She frowned. "So I don't get anything for trying, even if I give it my best?"

"Do they give gold medals to athletes just because they tried their best? You've got to cross the finish line."

She pursed her lips. Those fucking lips he wanted wrapped around his cock. Nevertheless, he didn't press her and let her take her time as she weighed the full brunt of her acceptance. This was her last chance to back out.

"All right, let's get started," she declared with impatience.

He scratched the stubble that had started to come in about his jaw. She sure wanted to talk to this Sam badly.

"You sound like you want this root canal over and done with."

"At least I know what a root canal entails."

Crossing to her, he chuckled. He grasped her by the chin. "I won't promise curtain number three won't be as miserable as a root canal for you, but if you let yourself, it could be a lot more enjoyable."

Defiance still shone in her eyes. She wanted to prove him wrong. But he had wrested orgasms from her before, so he could it again. He *would* do it again.

She couldn't know it, but her resistance made him more determined, made him more drawn to her. He ran his thumb across her cheeks and over her lips, drawing the bottom one down till they parted in the way that drove him crazy. She had pretty teeth. Even and white, a gleaming contrast to her darker skin.

"Don't worry, pet," he said softly. "You made a good choice."

Her eyes shimmered and lost some of their defiance. He released her and stepped back. Wordlessly, she stared at him, still wary like a mouse cornered by the cat. Did she think he would add to the bruise on her cheek, or did she remember what he had said he wanted to do with her—fuck her, torment her, and devastate her?

"Go sit on the bed," he instructed.

It wasn't what she wanted to hear. No matter. His sympathy only went so far because she should have thought of that before she signed up for the Scarlet Auction, and he was too selfish not to make use of his purchase, especially when he wasn't one who normally threw around two hundred thousand dollars lightly. Of course he would honor the safety word if she used it, but he was confident he could push her to edge without going too far.

He narrowed his eyes when she didn't comply right away. Did she not learn her lesson on that already? She read his expression, squared her shoulders and stalked over to the bed.

At the dresser, he pulled out the silk kerchief she had picked out from the thrift store. He folded it till it would serve nicely as a blindfold.

"What's that for?" she asked when he stood before her.

"What do you think it's for?" he replied.

"Is it necessary?"

"Doesn't matter if it is or isn't. Now, are you going to go with it or do you want it to be a long night? I can last the night. The question is, can you?"

Maybe it was a bit of a stretch saying he could last the night. Because he wanted Kimani so badly right now, he'd bust a nut if he had to wait the whole night. He could do it if he had to, to make good on his word, but it would be a long and torturous night for the both of them.

She remained still while he tied the silk kerchief over her eyes. Her breath grew shallow.

"Lie down," he told her.

After a pause, she held her towel and flopped backwards onto the bed. The move was hardly sexy. She looked as if she were getting ready for her annual gynecology exam. But her demeanor would change soon enough. He would see to that.

"Scoot up," he instructed.

Doing so meant lifting her legs. He

thought about reminding her that he had already seen just about every inch of her but decided to let her wallow in her discomfort. Fear, in the right dose and place and time, could have aphrodisiac qualities.

She placed her feet near her arse to conceal as much as possible and pushed herself toward the top of the bed. Back at the dresser, he took out the ties he'd purchased.

"I'm going to tie you to the bed," he said. "Nothing too challenging tonight."

The sleigh beds and simple rectangular headboards of modern beds were less fun to tie a person to than the four-post bed he had in his penthouse in San Francisco, but this camelback headboard had two small posts on either side, enough to bind the ties to. He took her left wrist, the one that wasn't clinging to her towel, and gently wound a tie around her. She looked like she had difficulty swallowing.

"You've been tied up before," he assumed.

"Not by a stranger," she replied with a slight hitch in her breath.

He tied the other end to the post. "Does that make it more exciting for you?"

"It makes me more nervous."

"Nervous in a good way?"

"I don't know. It could go either way. This could turn out g—"

He had taken her other wrist.

"—good or bad," she finished, not fighting him when he began to bind her right wrist to the other bedpost.

"It could," he acknowledged, "and you have a lot to do with it."

"So you say, but...you've shown you can be an asshole sometimes."

He threw open the towel, laying her entirely bare. She tensed and strained against the ties.

"I don't know that I would do that if I were you," he said, "especially when you're tied up and completely at my mercy. Now you're just inviting me to be an asshole."

His gaze took in everything from the nipples that had hardened as quickly as his cock had, to that sexy indent traversing the center of her midsection, to the gorgeous patch of hair at the base of her pelvis.

Damn. He might be the one in trouble. He grasped a breast, sinking his fingers into the flesh, remarkably soft and pliant given how firm her baps looked. There was so much he could to this orb. So much wickedness. Her dark-chocolate areolas were so fucking hot.

He brushed his thumb over the erect nipple. He pinched and pulled it hard enough to make her cry out.

"Expect an asshole, get an asshole," he warned.

"You're not always one," she said quickly. "Sometimes you're—you're a nice guy."

If he were a nice guy, he'd say things to reassure her, let her know he'd take good care of her. But he didn't feel like being nice right now. Partly because he wanted to fuck her till she couldn't see straight.

He cupped her throat, just below the chin. "You really believe that?"

She stretched her neck as if trying to get away from his grip, but his large hand easily encircled her. He could feel her pulse throbbing beneath his thumb.

"You were nice to me yesterday—really nice," she affirmed. "And today. You didn't have to take me shopping."

He didn't. But there were things he had wanted to get in town, like the ties. Except for the condoms that were always in his suitcase, he hadn't brought anything fun with him to the cabin because he hadn't expected to be with anyone. But he could have let her make do with the sweats he had lent her yesterday or have her go naked 24/7 like the other women.

But he had wanted to put her at ease. Which he shouldn't have had to do. She was supposed to be a sure thing. She had sold herself as a fucktoy, after all, and he fully expected to be satisfied with his purchase.

CHAPTER TEN

Was this the right choice? Kimani wondered. Maybe she should have tried harder to cajole him into letting her use his cellphone. What kind of guy doesn't accept a ready blow job? She hadn't wanted to perform one, let alone offer it, but a blow job would have been less nerve-racking than curtain number three, even if it contained no penetration.

She wanted to swallow but didn't dare with his hand fastened around her throat.

Jesus, you're such a wimp. He hasn't even done much yet.

The operative word being "yet," she argued with herself. Why did he have to grasp her throat, perhaps the most vulnerable part of her body? Was he going to choke her? Was he into asphyxiation?

She forced herself to breathe to calm her nerves and take responsibility. She had chosen this. He hadn't forced it on her.

A minor point. He put you between a rock and a hard place.

But it didn't do any good to blame him. She wanted to call Sam, and curtain number three was the only path Ben offered. Provided Ben could be trusted. But he hadn't given any indication that he would go back on his word.

That can change. Just give him time. Maybe he says the right things because he knows what you want to hear. That's what's so messed up about this situation. You can't wholly trust him, but you don't truly have a choice not to.

To her relief, he released her throat. His hand slid to her sternum. Without sight, her attention became laser-focused on his touch. She could feel every millimeter where his skin came in contact with hers. His hand continued between her breasts. Her nipple still smarted from when he had pinched and yanked it. The motherfucker. That had hurt. She hoped he wouldn't do it again but braced herself in case he did.

But his hand continued its journey downward, his digits lightly sweeping over her midsection, around her navel, and through the curls at her mound. Her breath grew shallow. Her nerves hopped and pinged like droplets of water hitting oil in a frying pan. And inside of her, a molten warmth percolated.

Though her thighs were pressed together, he found his way between them and cupped her folds.

Jesus, I'm making a mess of my scoop...

"When do I get to touch you?" she asked. Maybe it wasn't too late to find a way out, a way to get him to come before he could do too much. Once he'd come, he'd be comatose, or at least drowsy, like the rest of his gender. She could avail herself of his cell then.

He stroked her flesh. "Do you want to touch me?"

"You don't like to answer questions, do you?"

"You ask a lot of questions."

"I guess I'm inquisitive."

"Yes, you are."

He sounded thoughtful, but she was becoming less so as her body responded to the caress of his long fingers along her labia, teasingly close to her clit. Her body, remembering how good he had made her feel earlier and yesterday, wriggled against his hand.

"I see you like that."

Not liking that he had noticed, she tensed her body against the arousal he coaxed. He had suggested she'd be begging for penetration. She'd have to be incredibly wound up and desperate to do that. Although, if anyone could get her that way, it would probably be him. If she wanted a chance at completing curtain number three, she should probably stay as cool and collected as possible.

His middle finger insinuated itself between her folds to find her clit. He dragged his finger along that traitorous bud so very slowly.

Oh, Jesus. How did a guy of his size and build have such a delicate touch?

"Like that?" he cooed into her ear.

You know damn well I do. Aloud, she replied, "You like teasing your women?"

He chuckled. "The thing is, you have to answer my questions."

"Why?"

"Because there are consequences if you don't. So how much do you like your clit being played with?"

"A little."

"Only a little?" There was a faint threat in his tone, indicating he wouldn't like it if she lied.

"I'm a little preoccupied."

"With what?"

"With what the rest of curtain number three entails."

He seemed to accept that as truth. "I said if you let yourself, you could enjoy it. So let yourself. Like you did yesterday."

"I don't know if my idea of what's enjoyable is the same as yours."

"It may not be, but I'll find out what makes you tick. I found some sweet spots yesterday, didn't I?"

With that, he fondled her a little more intently. Behind the silk kerchief, she closed her eyes and took a fortifying breath.

"Didn't I?" he asked sternly.

"Yes," she whispered. "If there's no penetration, what do you get out of this? I could give you a hand job but..." She yanked gently on her bonds to complete the sentence. "In fact, I'm pretty good at hand jobs."

"Yeah?"

"I once got a guy to come in sixty seconds."

"Maybe he had poor stamina."

"Maybe. Or maybe I'm that good. Wanna see how fast I can make you come?"

His breath deepened. She got excited that she had affected him in the same way he affected her.

But he made her pay for that. His finger swirled against her clit and settled in the spot that had driven her crazy on the patio yesterday evening. He stroked her slow and steady.

After a moment of silence, he said, "I don't come like most guys."

"What do you mean you 'don't come like most guys?'"

She was beginning to wonder if he had some kind of deformity. Is that why he hadn't shown her his cock yet?

"You'll see. I only tell you 'cause you may want to watch what you brag about."

"Are you the only one allowed to brag?"

"It's not bragging if it's an objective truth."

"Then I'm not bragging."

He paused his fondling. She wondered what he was thinking.

"All right," he said, pressing and rolling her clit in a way that made her womanhood clench. "I'll give you your chance. *After* we're done with curtain number three."

Damn. She had hoped he would untie her and remove the blindfold. Shivers of delight were zinging all the way to her toes, and wetness seeped through her slit. Her damn body wanted to respond to him. At this rate, she wasn't going to be able to hold out for long. Maybe she could keep her arousal at bay by focusing on something mundane, like what bills she had to pay and when was the last time she had balanced her checkbook? Or she could think about things that turned her off—like Jake Whitehurst and the creep that beat up Marissa.

A quick squeeze to her breast jolted her attention back to Ben.

"Spread 'em," he commanded, his hand pulling on her thigh.

Quickly, she drew her legs apart.

Jesus. She was spread, naked, and tied. This could not be further from what she had imagined.

The mattress sank and elevated as he shifted his weight and moved. What was coming next?

She felt his hands on her legs, keeping them apart. He had said there would be no penetration. So what was he doing?

Her legs jerked instinctively toward each other when she felt the brush of his lips on an inner thigh, but he held her in place.

Crap. He was down there.

He kissed his way along her thigh to her vulva. Anticipation fluttered in her belly. Would he go down on her? Should she let him? Was it safe? Wise? She half hoped he was a shitty eater.

She heard him inhale her scent, then felt his breath on her intimacy. It had been over a year since a guy had gone down on her. She actually didn't care too much for it because most men didn't know how to eat pussy. She had given her last boyfriend props for trying, though she'd found what he'd done down there a little odd. He had later explained that he was trying to write the alphabet with his tongue because he'd read about it in some men's magazine.

She nearly arched off the bed when Ben licked her, slow and deliberate. Did she really want to submit to this? He hadn't even touched her clit, but a tongue was so much more intimate than the hand.

"Relax," he said, pressing her back into the bed.

She tried peering through the blindfold. Unsuccessful, she allowed her head to fall back among the pillows. This could prove to be a long night.

His tongue toyed and teased, caressing all but that most important rosebud, almost as if he didn't know better. But she knew it was just a ruse, and it was driving her crazy. She tried to grind herself against him so his tongue would slip past her folds to her clit. He obliged, and his tongue grazed her clit ever so slightly. It was like a small ray of sunlight had escaped through the clouds.

She moaned.

"You want more?"

She didn't answer. Her body felt like a violin string drawn taut over the instrument. If she retreated from her arousal, it would be uncomfortable but possible. If she said yes, there would be no turning back.

His hands caressed her legs, up the backs of them to cup her ass before moving to her hips. She wanted him to touch her *there*, to make her come, make her squirt.

He feathered kisses on her inner thighs, then licked the crease where her thigh met her pelvis. "Well, pet?"

She groaned.

"Is that a yes?"

She muttered, "Yes."

"Ask me."

She drew in a shaky breath. "Please, I'd

like more."

You caved.

But the reward was worth it. His fingers parted her labia, and he applied his tongue earnestly to her clit. He came at her from different angles, with different motions, till he found the direction that elicited the greatest reactions. For her, it was side to side. And he didn't just confine himself to the surface of her clit. It was as if his tongue probed the interior of the bud, provoking something deeper and lower, sending shivers to her extremities. Then his mouth clamped down on the sensitive side, and he sucked.

O.M.G.

She couldn't believe it. It was more intense than her vibrator, more focused. He pulsed his sucking, and it felt *so damn good...*

"You taste good, pet," he said with a teasing flick of the tongue.

No, don't stop.

But the mattress moved as he pushed himself up.

"Now where did I put those candles?" he asked himself.

Candles? What the...

She heard him moving around, then

heard him return to the bed. He had found the candles, she suspected.

"You like to get kinky with candles?" She tried a mocking tone but it came out nervous.

"You'll see," he replied.

Great. Why the hell did I agree to this?

He wrapped a tie around her right ankle before pulling it toward one corner of the bed. After securing her right leg, he tied her left ankle to the opposite corner. There was enough slack in the ropes to allow her to bend her knees slightly but not enough to close her thighs.

"Fuck me," he whispered to himself.

He trailed a hand from one ankle, up the calf, the side of her leg, over her hip, and across her belly. His fingers gently combed her pubic hair before caressing below.

There was no thinking of mundane matters now. Her mind was firmly focused on the area between her legs. A faint smell of orange spice wafted to her. And when he stroked her clit with his finger, she was sure she could come within minutes. He fondled her till she could no longer contain her panting and moaning.

This is not going well.

His hand was on a breast.

He groped the orb, rolled it over her chest, then passed his thumb over the nipple. Despite the light touch, she gasped. His thumb and forefinger pinched the side of her breast.

She gave a small cry. Something warm and slick dripped onto her skin. He caressed and rubbed. Was that one of those massage candles? They'd been in a box, but she hadn't looked at them beyond noticing that.

This was too much. She struggled a bit, but like his massage the other day, he was rubbing away her resistance. Over and over, he smoothed the oil onto her, finding new sensitive spots and areas that made her groan and writhe. Then he increased his attentions to her sensitive breasts. His nibbling and suckling were wreaking havoc on her senses. He pinched and rolled her other nipple with his fingers.

This is too much.

His other hand reached below and stroked her clit. The percolation of pleasure there made the other sensations more bearable, taking the edge off the heat of the massage and what he did to her nipples. When he backed off the pressure to the nipples, she found herself arching her back, seeking his mouth.

He pushed himself off the bed, leaving her bereft once more. Her clit pulsed for his touch. She heard him unzip his fly.

He was taking off his clothes. Her heartbeat quickened. She heard another zipper. From his suitcase maybe? The crinkle of plastic. The tearing of plastic. What else did he have in mind? What else had he bought in town today?

The bed sank with his weight. She could sense the warmth of his body between her legs. A pillow was pulled beneath her butt, lifting and angling her pelvis.

"No penetration," he said.

His knees pressed against her thighs, keeping them apart. Then something hard and rounded touched her clit.

His penis. The sound of plastic had been a condom wrapper.

His fingers had felt great on her, but the diameter of his cock was exquisite. His tip traced the length of her clit, stopping just above the opening from which her moisture had leaked and trickled down her ass cheeks. Her pussy clenched at his nearness, and for a second, she wanted him inside.

He drew his cock up and down her clit,

the tip teasing her slit every time.

"Feeling good?"

She moaned. "Yes..."

He rubbed his erection along her folds. She couldn't take it anymore. Wanting to come badly, she ground herself on his thick and hardened shaft. He placed a hand on her pelvis to still her motions as he withdrew.

After a tense moment, as her body screamed in protest at the deprivation, she swallowed her pride and said, "Please don't stop."

"You want to come, pet?"

"Yes."

"You want me to fuck you?"

"Yes. Please."

To her relief and joy, she felt his cock pushing against her labia, making her quiver. The promise of release made her clit throb even more. He remembered the most sensitive spot on her clitoris and agitated the head of his cock there.

She came unhinged, her body erupting in shudders, euphoria flooding her body.

He stayed where he was, his cock milking every spasm from her body until her clit became too sensitive. Withdrawing, he left her wanting more. "My turn, pet."

How did he intend to come? If he was going to keep her tied up but not penetrate her, was he going to jack himself off?

He caressed the other side of her clit with his cock. The discomfort was mild, and it wasn't long before a familiar warmth began to bloom. The afterglow of her orgasm hadn't dissipated, and his stroking soon had the embers flaring anew. When he returned his cock to that sensitive spot, she found herself on a beautiful plateau of pleasure, from which the only way off would be another orgasm, though she would be content to remain in the rapturous limbo because it felt so damn good.

He rubbed himself against her a little harder, grunting several times. She felt him shake against her. He was coming. Damn. She wanted him to keep going. Maybe he would be generous enough to masturbate her with his hand or untie her so she could do it herself.

Pausing, he grunted louder. His legs twitched against hers. But to her surprise, he resumed pushing his cock against her. Any second she expected his cock to grow soft, but he remained hard. She could only guess that he hadn't come after all. She, on the other hand, was close to another climax.

"Yes. Oh, God, yes," she breathed.

So close. So very close.

But he didn't speed up or go harder like most guys would. He kept his pace and pressure steady, forcing her to climb higher and higher to reach the pinnacle she desired so that when she reached her climax, it flowed long and glorious.

CHAPTER ELEVEN

She was so fucking hot when she came. He couldn't hold it any longer. He dug his cock into that two o'clock spot on her clit and allowed the ejaculation to follow his second orgasm. He had thought he could hold out for a longer, more prolonged orgasm, but the sight of her completely giving in to her orgasm had curtailed his chances.

But there were still five days left to the week. Plenty of time. He only hoped she could last that long, because he intended to use her body till there was nothing left.

Leaning over her, he stared at her nether lips, imagining his cock sliding between them. There was so much he wanted to do with her, *to* her. Five days might not be enough.

A final shiver went through her before she asked, "Do I get to use the phone now?"

"We're done with curtain number three," he acknowledged. He would have stayed where he was, hovering over her body, enjoying her nearness, but her limbs might be sore. Pulling off the condom and tossing it into the wastebasket, he got off the bed. "But there's something else I want." He palmed a breast.

She objected, "Greedy, much?"

He trapped the nipple between his middle and forefinger and pulled upward, stretching the little bud. She gasped, her lips parting wide.

Gently, he pinched her nipple between thumb and forefinger, then started to twist the perky nub. It didn't take long before she was squirming.

"Okay, okay!" she cried. "What do you want?"

He released the nipple.

She was glaring at him through the blindfold. He was pretty sure her eyes looked at him in the same way they had when they'd first met, when Jake had her and Claire kneel for three hours on the living room floor. Kimani's eyes were very expressive, and he had read their message loud and clear: *Fuck you.*

Were her eyes sending the same words right now? Or did they call him an asshole?

It didn't matter. He was going to turn her message around and, before long, have her screaming *fuck me.*

"I want you to give up control to me," he answered.

"And why should I do that?"

"Because I'm good."

"Good at what?"

Lightly, he traced the underside of a breast. "Good at finding your buttons. Good at making you come."

In telling reluctance, she pursed her lips. He waited patiently. He wasn't going to force her to say anything. Her consent, her willing admission, was far more challenging—and arousing.

"You said I could get your phone if I chose what's behind curtain number three," she objected.

"And you've earned the privilege of using it. *When* you get my mobile is another matter."

She shook her head in exasperation. "You're just making shit up on the go."

He passed his hand over her toned midriff. "You don't have to like it."

"You don't have to be such an asshole."

"Were you lying when you said you were up for anything?"

"The honorable thing to do would be to lay out the expectations ahead of time so I know what I'm getting myself into."

His nostrils flared. He could handle being called an asshole—or even an airy-fairy pussy—but having his honor called into question was grounds for fighting. His hand had slid to her mound, and he resisted twisting his fingers viciously into the curls there.

He could have replied "maybe" just to emphasize the point he had made not ten seconds ago—that she *was* at his complete whim—but he decided not to be a complete tosser.

Again she frowned. It only made him want to fuck her mouth more.

"If you want to call Sam," he continued, "say 'I'm yours.'"

Her cheeks flushed and she flinched when he caressed the inside of her thigh.

"Ugh," she grunted beneath her breath but not quietly enough.

He slapped her inner thigh and decided he would be a tosser after all. "What was that?"

"I'm yours," she mumbled, but he heard the sincerity there, and what it had maybe cost her to say it aloud.

The words lit a fire through his veins. Blood rushed to his groin, bringing new life to his cock.

"Good," he said. "I'm going to untie you, and you're going to stand next to the bed."

He took in a long breath to calm his ardor before untying her from the corners of the bed. He removed the blindfold before pulling her to her feet. He turned her around to face the bed and so she could see herself in the floor-to-ceiling mirrors that formed the closet doors.

He cupped her mound and rubbed his fingers against her wetness. She shivered. Good. Her body was up for more.

He took a step back to admire her backside. Looking at her arse cheeks, so full and round, gave him a complete hard-on. He bent her over the bed, her arse rounding the edge nicely.

Standing behind her, he cradled a sphere. She was so bloody enticing, she begged to be ravished. But he had promised no penetration. He kneaded the buttock, grinding his thumb into her gluteus maximus before playfully backhanding it. It quivered only slightly. He massaged the other cheek, warming it up and trying to work away the tension.

He could tell she was nervous, so he reached between her thighs and stroked her cunt lips. She was still nice and juicy down there. Her breath became uneven.

"This Sam sure is important to you," he remarked as he slid his fingers along her wet and slick flesh.

"She is."

She was still going with the lie that Sam was a girl.

"She's a really good friend," she added, "and I just don't want her to worry about me."

"So you told her what you're up to?"

He was pretty sure the nondisclosure agreement she had to sign with the Scarlet Auction precluded her from talking about it with anyone.

"I didn't tell her much, just that I was off to have sex with a stranger for a week. But she worries a lot."

"That's all you told her?"

"Yes, that's all I told her."

That was another lie. He didn't like being lied to, but he would address that at a later time.

His fingers grazed her clitoris, still plump and engorged. She moaned. He continued working her, giving her more of what she wanted. Groaning, she ground into his touch as he flicked his finger back and forth over her clit.

Satisfied, he worked her sweet spot harder. She climaxed an instant later. He ground her orgasm into her clit. Her body convulsed violently. Still holding her in place, he slid his erection between her blushing arse cheeks. He rubbed her moisture on his shaft and dry humped her backside while her arousal settled back to a simmer.

So close. He was so close to her. It was enough to make him come again. He decided he would. Reaching beneath her, he squeezed a breast as he shot his load onto her ass cheeks. Shivers wracked his body. Still thrusting, he grabbed himself and squeezed the last of his orgasm out.

A shudder shook his head. Maybe it was all the pent-up ardor, but he hadn't come like that in a while. He hadn't been able to hold off his ejaculation, and he wondered if this unusual lapse in control should concern him.

CHAPTER TWELVE

Kimani could feel his legs trembling against hers as she remained halfway on the bed, her derrière rounding its edge. His cum on her ass had done nothing to diminish the rapture of her orgasm. Quite the contrary, everything he'd done had intensified the sensations. His cum, wet and sticky, pooled on her lower back. He could have penetrated her, and she would've been relatively helpless to stop him, but he had kept his word.

She would have been content to lay as she was against the soft sheets of the bed, waiting for the throbbing between her legs to settle, but a knock sounded at the door.

"Sod off—beat it," Ben grunted.

"Jake says it's time for the sluts to go downstairs," Vince said through the door.

"I'm not done with mine."

She started. Not done? As good as her

orgasms had been, she wasn't sure she could take any more. And there was something else she needed to do. What was it? Oh yeah, call Sam.

"I'm locking up, so the little ladies need to be down there now," Vince said.

Ben pushed himself away from the bed, ready to confront Vince.

"Wait," she said. She didn't want to miss out on the opportunity to talk freely with the other women. "I want to go down."

Ben returned a hard stare. "I'm not done yet."

She sat up and couldn't resist looking at his crotch. She had felt his length rubbing her, so she knew he wasn't a eunuch—not even close. And there wasn't any deformity that she could see. She wondered what it would have felt like to have him inside her...

Realizing he saw the direction of her gaze, she quickly looked up and cleared her throat. "Please. I'm not sure I'm up for much more tonight. We can continue tomorrow. I promise I'll be good—very good tomorrow."

He crossed his arms in thought. "What about your call to Sam?"

"I'll make it quick. Tell Vince I just need ten minutes."

He approached her, lifted her chin, and ran his thumb along her bottom lip. She could smell herself upon his hand. His gaze went from her lips and bore deep into her eyes. "You had better be bloody good."

Her pulse quickened, but she replied, "I promise."

Already she regretted what she had gotten herself into, but it had to be done. She was here on a mission to get the scoop that would launch her career. She had to remember that, no matter how distracting Ben could be.

"She'll be down in ten minutes," Ben told Vince.

"Ten minutes," Vince confirmed.

His footsteps retreated down the hall. Ben got a damp towel and wiped the cum off her back, and then presented her with his cellphone.

"Thank you," she said, taking the phone into the bathroom.

After closing the door, she pulled on new underwear and Ben's shirt from yesterday, ran the leave-in conditioner through her hair as quickly as she could before wrapping it up in the scarf he had used to blindfold her, and brushed her teeth before finally calling Sam.

"I've only got a few minutes," she told him quietly.

"It's pretty messed up that the auction took your cellphone," Sam said. "Are you still doing okay?"

Was she okay? All that Ben had done to her just now flashed through her mind. Her clit still tingled. As did her nipples. And there was more to come. She had promised to be good tomorrow. Shit.

"Yeah, I'm fine," she lied.

"Good, but anytime you start to feel unsafe, you let me know. I'll drive up there myself if I have to."

"I'm getting this story for you," she affirmed, in case he doubted her resolve.

"You think you can get more on this Benjamin Lee? His family has got their thumb in a lot of developments in the area. Except for the waterfront property in Oakland, they're usually not the lead, but they're the prominent financial backers."

"Is that so strange? The Chinese finance a lot of things."

"But how many of them have a family member who's running for mayor of Oakland?"

"That doesn't mean there's anything

shady going on."

"We won't know unless we look. Was Benjamin the only Lee that was at the auction?"

"He wasn't at the auction at all. He's working with one of the guys here who was, though."

"Are you sure he didn't have anything to do with the auction?"

She furrowed her brow. "I guess I don't know for sure. His cousin was at the auction."

She heard a knock at the bedroom door, followed by Vince's voice.

"I think my time is up," she told Sam.

""Well, find out what you can and keep me posted. Do you know when you can check in again tomorrow?"

"I don't." She recalled her promise to Ben about being good. "Probably late in the day."

She said goodbye and walked out of the bathroom.

"Thanks for letting me use your phone," she said to Ben, who looked unfairly sexy in a plain white t-shirt and gray shorts.

"You've earned it," he replied.

"I'd like to use it again tomorrow."

"That shouldn't be a problem if you make

good on your promise."

She was afraid of that. Aloud, she said, "Good night."

She opened the door to find Vince waiting for her. She followed him down to the basement where the other women had already gotten into bed.

"See you ladies in the morning," Vince smirked before shutting the door behind him and locking it.

Kimani pulled out the dress from her bag of purchases. "I bought you a dress, in case you're allowed to wear one."

"I can't believe you got to go shopping," Lisa said to Kimani. "You totally lucked out. You got the nicest guy, at least out of the four here."

"Yeah, but nice guys are boring," said Ryan.

"You're not saying you like jerks better?" asked Kimani.

"Hell yeah. They are way more exciting."

"Jake's definitely got some bad boy in him," said Claire with a smile.

"Bad boys are fun in fiction, but would you really want to be involved with one in real life?" Kimani inquired as she got into bed.

Ryan rolled her eyes. "Of course he's not

going to be all jerk, but he definitely needs to be alpha."

"And nice is incompatible with alpha?"

"Pretty much."

"I like nice guys," said Lisa as she rubbed lotion over her slender legs. "I'd rather be treated as a princess. Nice guys are good at that."

"How about being treated like a normal human being?" Kimani offered.

Ryan groaned. "Again, *boring.*"

"So what did you get to do besides shopping?" asked Claire.

"We toured a historic site, the Joss House. It's one of the oldest Taoist temples in the state."

"I thought you were going to say that you fucked each other's brains out in his car," Ryan said.

"No, we got pulled over by a CHP officer."

"Bummer."

"What did *you* guys get to do?"

"Had sex, of course."

Kimani looked over at Claire. "Was it fun?"

"It was okay," sighed Lisa as she snuggled under the covers. "I just wish my guy would last a little longer."

Ryan agreed, "I was this close to coming, then Derek came first. But I'm used to taking care of myself. I can't imagine not getting off. I mean, why else have sex?"

"Sometimes it feels good just to make out. It can be romantic."

"I'd take an orgasm over romance any day."

Kimani turned to Claire. "How was it for you?"

Claire furrowed her brow. "I think it's because I'm still new at this, but is sex usually uncomfortable?"

"Uncomfortable in what way?"

"Jake likes to fuck hard." Claire giggled. "Just like Christian Gray in *Fifty Shades*."

"I love it hard," said Ryan.

"It doesn't hurt for you? Sometimes?"

"I don't like it hard," said Lisa. "It feels like I'm getting a cramp if the guy is too hard with me. Maybe it's because I've got such a petite body."

"Did you say anything to Jake about it?" Kimani asked Claire.

Claire nodded. "I told him it hurt. He said, 'Hurts good, doesn't it, babe?'"

"What did you say then?"

"Nothing. I didn't want him to be upset or

disappointed. I want my bonus."

Kimani had forgotten about the bonus, mainly because she hadn't expected to collect on any money.

"How much is the bonus?"

"Ten percent if our buyers are pleased at the end of the week," said Lisa. "I think I'll finally buy myself a Prada handbag."

"I'm taking myself to Hawaii with my bonus. What about you?" Ryan asked Kimani.

"I hadn't thought that far," Kimani replied.

"I meant, do you like a hard fucking?"

"It depends."

"That's such a boring non-answer."

"What does it depend on?" Claire inquired.

"Sometimes it feels good, sometimes it doesn't," Kimani answered. "Maybe it depends on how aroused I am or the angle of penetration."

Claire seemed to store away that bit of information.

"If what Jake does doesn't feel good, you should let him know. Do you have a safety word in place?"

"Safety word?"

"We're all supposed to have safety words. That's what we say when we want the guys— our buyers—to stop doing something because it doesn't feel good. Did any of you guys get safety words?"

"I know what a safety word is," said Ryan. "But I don't think they're absolutely necessary. Derek knows what I'm into and what I'm not. I filled out that long-ass questionnaire for the Scarlet Auction people."

"Don't you think it's good to have a safety word on hand? What if he does something in a way that doesn't work for you?"

Ryan snuggled into her pillow and closed her eyes. "You worry too much, honey."

The rest of the women looked ready to call it a night as well, but Kimani pressed, "It doesn't bother any of you that you don't have safety words?"

"Jake did say things are going to get more intense tomorrow," Claire said, knitting her brows in thought.

"Did he elaborate?"

"Just that it was going to be a lot of fun."

Fun for whom? Kimani wondered wryly.

CHAPTER THIRTEEN

"So what did you find out?" Ben asked. His toothbrush hung out the side of his mouth because he had picked up the call in the middle of brushing his teeth.

"Her full name is Kimani Morgan Taylor," Stephens, on speakerphone, answered. "Born in San Francisco. Like you said, she went to Stanford and got a bachelor's degree in communications. 3.8 GPA. Then went to journalism school at Berkeley. Currently works for a boutique financial firm called Stone & Young Financial Services on Montgomery Street. She's an administrative assistant there."

Ben spit into the sink. "Did you say journalism school?"

"Yeah, and get this: I pulled up her transcript—"

"I didn't ask you to do that."

"I know, but I like to be thorough. And when you had me look up that Sam Green guy, I remembered reading in one of his bios that he was a guest lecturer at Berkeley. And guess what?"

"Kimani took a class from him."

"Bingo."

"Why is she working at a financial firm then?" Ben wondered aloud.

"My guess is that she couldn't get a job in the field she wanted."

"You find anything out else about her and Sam?"

"Either she's really good or he liked her. A lot. She got an A+ in his class."

Ignoring the brief pang of jealousy, Ben took Stephens off speakerphone as he walked out of the bathroom. "I want you to find everything you can on Kimani Taylor and the Scarlet Auction."

"Scarlet Auction? What's that?"

"An exclusive service where women sell themselves to rich assholes for a week."

"Rich asshole like you, boss?" Stephens chortled.

"Just get me something by tomorrow."

"I'll have Sanjiv do some hacking. He should be up and about right now since it's early afternoon in Singapore."

"Good."

Stephens would produce. He always did. And Ben liked that Stephens didn't ask nosy questions. The man didn't need to know the why, just the what, then figured out how. He knew that if Ben needed him to know more, it was up to Ben to tell him.

"Oh, and Rosenstein wants to know if two million will be enough?" Stephens asked.

"No coordination, remember? The PAC has to run completely independent from Uncle Gordon's campaign. Get that through Rosenstein's thick head."

"Got it."

Ben shook his head. The group of developers who had met regarding the Oakland mayoral election should never have allowed Rosenstein to head up the independent expenditure to support Gordon's candidacy.

Ben threw himself onto the bed, and his thoughts immediately turned to Kimani. Though he hadn't been too happy when Vince interrupted them earlier, he wasn't one to dwell on what could've been. It was probably better that she went anyway. He probably would have been tempted to go further than she was comfortable with.

He didn't get it. He didn't like the agitation she generated in him. What was it about her?

Just thinking about her was giving him a hard-on. He adjusted himself. If he kept thinking about her, he wasn't going to get to sleep anytime soon.

So he thought about his meeting with Tyrell Jenkins. His secretary had been able to set up an appointment for next week. That was at least one good outcome from his association with Jake. That and Kimani.

Fuck. He was back to thinking about her again.

Rubbing his temples, he forced his mind to Uncle Gordon's campaign. He had told his uncle that he would put together a fundraiser with other developers in the area. It would probably only raise $50,000, given the city's campaign contribution limits. Gordon, a county planning commissioner, was up against a city councilmember, Richard Jessfield. The contribution limits were what had prompted Ben to throw out the idea of an independent expenditure campaign, which didn't have the same limitations that a candidate's campaign committee had to operate under. Jessfield had already raised the max amount of nearly half a million. Another viable contender, although currently in third, was an Oakland school board member, Linda Wong. It was expected that Wong and Gordon would end up splitting the Asian vote, leaving Jessfield the winner.

Ben remembered the conversation he had overheard Kimani having with Sam on the phone last night. Why did Kimani have an interest in the Oakland mayoral race? Did she have a side job freelancing for Sam? Was she working on a story? But how did the Scarlet Auction fit into this?

Ben decided not to dwell on questions that had no affirmative answers. He would know all that he needed to know soon enough.

His thoughts wandered to the vision of her arse rounding the edge of the bed. So fucking fly. He imagined sinking himself into her pussy, pounding into her, his pelvis slapping into those succulent buttocks, his cock buried deep in her wetness.

With a frustrated grunt, he resorted to the mantra he'd used to block out the pain when he got beat up by his gang brothers as part of the initiation. He had not been allowed to defend himself as they punched, kicked, and took a cane to him. He hadn't needed to use the mantra since. But it helped settle him enough to fall asleep.

The next morning, he awoke shortly before receiving a text from Stephens:

CHECK YOUR EMAIL

Ben finished up his sequence of *tai chi chuan* before picking up his phone. Stephens had sent him a couple of files related to the Scarlet Auction. There were legal documents that Kimani signed, including an extensive NDA; a record of her payment to the Scarlet Auction—the "processing" fee; a detailed questionnaire on her sexual preferences and interests; and a brief assessment of her profile based on the questionnaire. The conclusion stated "Sexually adventurous, likes it when men are in charge, looking for fun, and is basically up for anything."

Up for anything? It sounded too good to be true. She didn't exactly exhibit the enthusiasm of someone who was up for anything.

maybe she just wasn't into it with him. No, given how quickly she had come for him, he doubted that to be entirely the case.

Fuck. This was more than anyone could hope for.

After taking a shower, he took care of a few work items. By the time he went downstairs, the other guys were already at the table having breakfast.

"My chef found a replacement," said Jake, "so the sluts don't have to cook today."

"Thank God," said Derek. "They weren't very good."

"Dig in," Jake said to Ben after dismissing the chef, a small middle-aged man who may or may not have been aware of what occurred at the cabin.

Ben grabbed himself a glass of water, then started some tea. "I'm good."

"This bacon's the bomb," said Derek with a mouthful.

"I don't need breakfast," Ben replied.

"What do you mean you don't need breakfast? It's the most important meal of the day."

"I like to go without."

"He does this weird eating regimen," said Jason. "It includes crazy shit like fasting."

"That *is* crazy shit. Why would you do that?"

Jason rolled his eyes. "Something about keeping your body pure."

"What? Dude, this is bacon. Fucking good bacon. Best invention ever."

Ben watched as Derek helped himself to another plateful. "Where are the women?"

"You mean the sluts," Jake rephrased. "I'll have Vince let them up after we've eaten."

"We gonna ski again today?" Derek asked.

"Sure, if you want to."

"What else you got planned?"

"Some fun with our purchases."

"Yeah? Like what?"

"You'll see."

The women came up fifteen minutes later. As usual, they were all naked, including Kimani, even though Ben had not specifically required her to go sans clothing 24/7. Almost immediately, he felt the need to adjust his crotch. A naked woman was a naked woman, and always a beautiful sight. But without doubt, her body appealed to him most. Lisa had a waif-like figure, slender and petite like that of a teenage girl. Claire, with her fake baps, looked top-heavy. Ryan and Kimani looked sturdy. Kimani was a little fuller in the arms and legs than Ryan and more defined due to her athleticism. Of the four women, she was the only one without makeup. Ryan had a touch of lip gloss, but Claire and Lisa had the full works with lots of eyeliner and mascara.

"Morning, sluts," Jake greeted. "You lucked out. You sluts don't have to make breakfast today. In fact, one of you will be lucky enough to get this."

He showed them a beautifully plated dish of French toast with creme anglaise, berries, and a drizzle of maple syrup. The eyes of all four women brightened at the sight.

"That's what the winner gets for breakfast," said Jake. "This is how it's going to work—"

"Before we begin—" said Kimani.

Jake glared in Ben's direction. "Didn't you teach your slut not to speak unless spoken to?"

"I didn't make that one of my rules," Ben replied.

Kimani raised her hand. "Permission to speak."

"Denied." "Granted."

Jake and Ben exchanged glances.

"What is it?" Ben asked Kimani.

"I just wanted to make sure we all had safety words," she answered. "The Scarlet

Auction said that we were expected to have safety words."

"Safety words, hunh?" Jake sneered. "You afraid of something, Slut #2?"

"It's good protocol. Just in case."

Jake turned to Claire. "You need a safety word, babe?"

"No, Sir," Claire replied.

"How about you, Slut #3?" Jake asked Ryan.

"I'm cool," said Ryan.

Jake looked over at Lisa, who shook her head.

Ben was about to intercede when Kimani said, "Mercy. We'll use 'mercy' as the safety word."

That was what he had given her for a safety word.

Jake turned his glare to Kimani. "You don't get to set the rules, Slut #2." He turned to Ben. "We're in charge, not them. Or do you need me to take over from you?"

"She's right," Benjamin said. "It *is* good protocol."

"Protocol? You guys want to take the fun out of this."

"Safety words can allow you to have more fun," Kimani offered.

"Whatever. You and Benji can have your safety word. The othersaren't so chicken."

Ben straightened. He had already told the asswipe that only his mother and sisters ever called him Benji.

Seeing Ben's displeasure, Jake put up his hands. "Sorry, man. I forgot again."

Jason intervened before Ben questioned Jake's forgetfulness. "So what do the chicks have to do to win breakfast?"

"First, they have to be good pets." He went to stand in front of Claire. "You're going to be my pet piggie."

She wrinkled her nose and raised her hand.

Jake pushed her down to all fours. "Piggies don't raise their hands. They don't have hands. They have hoofs. And they don't talk. They oink. Oink for me, my little piggie."

When Claire didn't respond right away, Jake snapped, "Oink for me."

"Oink," she murmured with her face down.

"You can do better than that."

"Oink, oink," she snorted.

"That's a good little piggie." Jake turned to the other guys. "What kind of pets do you have?"

Jason studied Lisa. "Mine is a pussycat. Come here, pussycat."

Lisa got on all fours, crawled to Jason, and rubbed up against his leg.

Derek walked over to Ryan. "What kind of pet do you want to be?"

"My favorite animals are horses," she answered, "so I would like to be a pony, Sir."

She got down on all fours and neighed.

Kimani turned to Ben, looking less than enthusiastic. She had promised him yesterday that she was going to be good. He was going to hold her to it.

CHAPTER FOURTEEN

A puppy dog," Ben said.
"That's perfect," said Jake.
"Slut #2 is going to be a bitch."

This is nice and degrading, Kimani thought to herself as she got down on all fours with reluctance. She had gotten over, mostly, having to be naked in front of these guys. Unlike Jake, Ben had not made nudity a requisite. She had decided to go without clothing in solidarity with the other women. But she would have willingly passed up pretending to be a four-legged animal. She couldn't even remember ever playing a pet as a child. She understood that petplay was kinky, and maybe if it was just her and Ben, it wouldn't be so bad.

Maybe.

"For the first test to earn your breakfast," Jake announced, "our pets must prove to us how good they are at being a pet. My piggie is going to roll around in the mud and oink like a happy pig."

Claire bit down on her lower lip, but with Jake staring at her intently, she wasn't going to disobey. She lay on her back and rolled from side to side.

"Oink, oink," she squeaked.

Lisa licked her arms like a cat cleaning itself and meowed.

"Mine is giving me a pony ride," Derek said. He sat astride Ryan's back, pretending he was a cowboy with a lasso. "Yeehaw!"

With dread, Kimani looked up at Ben. What was he going to make her do?

"I would make that bitch lick our shoes," suggested Jake.

Ben looked at him. "She's not your pet anymore. She's *mine*."

He scanned the room before saying to her, "Fetch me that pen on the floor by the plant."

Shit. How had he seen that? She had deliberately placed the pen there after arriving in the room. The recorder inside of it was on.

"Go on. Fetch."

Suppressing a scowl, she crawled on all fours over to the pen and picked it up with her mouth. Crawling back, she dropped the pen at his feet.

"Pick it up and put it in my hand," he instructed.

She did as told, hoping he wouldn't click the top of the pen, which would turn the recorder off.

"Good puppy," he said

"Don't dogs bark?" Jake asked.

Though Ben didn't look pleased with Jake's interjection, he turned to Kimani. "Are you a happy puppy, my pet?"

Fucker. He wanted her to bark.

"Woof."

She couldn't believe she had just done that. This story had better land her that job at the *Tribune*.

"Do you like fetching things for me?"

She ground her teeth before barking, "Woof, woof."

She noticed the tenting at his crotch. The guy was getting off on this shit.

"Now show me what other tricks you can do. Rollover."

Bastard. But she went to the floor and rolled over. He studied her with a cool, almost eerie intensity, but arousal dilated his dark pupils.

"Now sit up and beg."

She got up on her knees, put up her hands like two front paws, and panted.

Jake laughed. "Maybe you've got your pet trained well after all."

"Now wag your tail to show how happy you are."

Something about the way he looked at her, his I-want-to-fuck-you-now stare, messed with her. He was pleased with her performance, and that made her glad.

Jesus, what's wrong with me?

She got down on all fours and wiggled her ass.

"Good puppy."

"My kitty wants a ride on the pony," said Jason.

Derek got off of Ryan. "Be my guest."

Jason nodded at Lisa, who went to sit atop Ryan.

"Pussies don't sit up, do they?" asked Jason.

Lisa lay down along the length of Ryan's back. Derek gave Ryan's butt a swat. Ryan crawled around the room.

Jake went to the table and grabbed a plum from the basket of fruit. "Now, let's see who's the best at fetch. Is it the piggie, the pony, the kitty or the bitch? Whoever brings me back the plum first earns a point towards breakfast."

I am not fetching for that asshole.

But when she looked at Ben, he raised his brows. "You're not planning to disappoint? You promised to be good today."

She didn't get it. She was pretty certain he didn't like Jake all that much. Why was he playing along?

Jake opened the door to the patio and tossed the plum out into the water. The French toast had looked scrumptious, but it wasn't worth this. And she loved French toast. Nevertheless, she had to put on a good show.

"What are you waiting for?" Jake asked the women. "Go fetch!"

They scrambled on all fours out the patio door and down the steps to the dock on the water. Ryan leapt into the cold water without hesitation. Kimani and Lisa followed, but Claire remained on the dock.

"This water's freezing!" Lisa cried.

Ryan swam to the floating plum, bit into it to secure it, and swam back to the dock. She pranced up back the stairs to the patio, where the men stood watching.

Derek raised both arms into the air.

"Yeah! My pet won!"

As if disappointed, Jake shook his head at the other women. "And I thought you girls were going to fight for it."

He turned to Jason, "Your pet talked. That's negative points."

Lisa, who barely had any flesh on her bones, still shivered from the cold lake.

"What's next?" asked Derek. "Do we get to fuck our pets yet?"

"Their next task is to suck us off and swallow every drop. Bonus points for the pet that sucks their guy off first."

Jake unbuttoned his shorts and pulled out his penis, which he presented to Claire. Jason, wearing board shorts, whipped his off in seconds. A trembling Lisa positioned herself on her knees in front of him. Ryan could barely wait for Derek to unzip his shorts.

Ben took out his semi-erect cock.

All eyes were upon him, sizing him up. Ryan looked ready to drool.

Jake gave a snort and turned back to Claire. "Get to work, piggie."

Kimani looked up at Ben, a warmth stirring in her loins when she saw the look he gave her, like he wanted to devour her. She wanted to taste his cock, but doing so without protection probably wouldn't be smart. How was she going to communicate without words that she wanted him to put on a condom?

"Good thing you promised to be good today," he murmured.

Did that mean he wasn't going to put on a condom?

"Woof, woof, woof," she tried, looking towards the direction of his bedroom.

"Your pet can't win if you leave," said Jake as he thrust his hips at Claire's face, making her choke.

"Ohhhhh, that feels good," moaned Jason from a few feet away.

His voice was joined by the sounds of Derek grunting and Ryan slurping.

"You guys are gonna have a lot of catching up to do," Jake observed to Ben.

Kimani barked once more in the direction of the bedroom, then at his cock, and back to the bedroom.

"Mercy," she said at last.

His face darkened. He wasn't pleased.

"This had better be good," he said.

"I'm willing to do the blow job," she explained, "but with a condom. We were told by the Scarlet Auction that all the men had been screened for STDs. Since you didn't go through the Auction protocols, I would feel safer with a condom."

"You got yourself a high-maintenance pet there," snickered Jake.

"I have condoms in my suitcase," Ben told her.

Beyond relieved, she said, "I'll make it up to you."

Resuming her role as a dog, she scrambled inside the cabin and up into his bedroom, where she found the condoms in his suitcase. Putting a packet in her mouth, she hustled back out onto the patio and offered it to Ben.

His cock was now fully erect. Last night, she had requested no penetration, though, towards the end, she had reconsidered her stance. She did want to know how it would feel to have him inside of her. Here was her chance. And she was going to make the most of it.

Once the condom was on, she fit her mouth over him and down as much of his length as she could. She sucked eagerly, a part of her regretting that she had to taste the rubber instead of him. She tried to swallow more and wished she had the use of her hands to massage his balls or search for his perineum. Though she didn't have a lot of deep-throating experience, she tried her best.

He gave an appreciative groan, a sound that thawed whatever resistance remained.

He fisted his hand in her hair and urged her down another inch. She had never felt so stuffed before. Her gag reflexes kicked in. He eased her off and allowed her a breather before guiding her back onto his rod of steel.

Beside her, Claire made all kinds of muffled choking sounds

Kimani dragged her tongue along Ben's cock, sucking him as hard as she could, till her cheeks grew sore. He gazed at her with an expression that spurred her to bear down harder on him. Arousing him excited her. She forgot the others and focused on Ben and the dark pools of his eyes as he gazed down at her.

"I'm gonna come!" cried Jason.

He pumped himself into Lisa's mouth. Coughing, she came off him. The last drops of his cum landed on her cheek.

It wasn't easy when there was so much of Ben to swallow, but Kimani resisted the urge to choke. By the clenching of his jaw and the quickening of his breath, she could tell he was close to coming. Just as he was about to come, he pulled her off him. His body jerked, his ab muscles tensed, and his eyes roll toward the back of his head. He was having an orgasm.

Or was he?

She expected the condom to fill with his semen, but it didn't. False alarm, she guessed. He guided her back onto his cock. By now, Derek had come as well.

"My pet swallowed every last drop!" he announced.

"That was yummy," said Ryan with a triumphant smile.

A few minutes later, Ben yanked Kimani's head back. He seemed to be coming again as small spasms went through his body. But his cock remained hard.

"Take it, piggie," Jake was screaming at Claire. "That's it. Take my fuckin' cock."

Claire was still struggling with choking, unable to keep up. Seconds later, he spurted his cum onto her face. She gasped for breath.

Jason and Derek had flopped into chairs. Lisa was trying to warm herself by rubbing her arms. Kimani tried to keep pace with Ben, who continued to push and pull the back of her head. She shouldn't have started out so fast and furious with the blow job. Like a rookie running a marathon, she had used up a lot of her energy at the beginning. But how was she to know that he would have trouble coming? Or was he deliberately holding off?

His fist tightened in her hair, which pulled at her scalp. Summoning up her energy, she sucked him as hard as she could to pull him over the edge. Once more, he slowed her down as it appeared he would finally climax. His brow furrowed. Shivers went through his body. He rolled his head back.

After collecting himself, he pushed her back onto his cock.

"Dude, you having some trouble?" asked Derek. "You can use my pet if you want. She gives a damn good blow job."

Ben thrust his hips in a more forceful rhythm. Left to her own devices, she would have given up or at least taken a rest, but she couldn't. His grip on her forced her to continue.

Unable to hold back the choking anymore, especially when he nearly shoved his whole length down her throat, she started heaving.

"Stay with me, pet," Ben encouraged.

Collecting herself, she tried. He bucked his hips faster until his climax bowled through him. His entire body tensed. The veins in his neck protruded. A flush spread across his chest. He gave several hard thrusts, and when he finally pulled out of her mouth, the condom was full of his cum.

"I came first, so that means my pet won," said Jason.

"But she didn't swallow every last drop," Derek objected.

Jake nodded and said to Jason, "Your pet had negative points coming in, so, all in all, I'd say the pony wins. Go help yourself to breakfast, Slut #3."

Claire looked crestfallen.

"Don't worry," Jake said, "the rest of you get to eat, too. Just nothing fancy. Follow me."

Her cheeks and jaw sore, Kimani wasn't sure she was up for the act of chewing. She watched Lisa and Claire crawl after Jake.

Jason came over to Ben. "Never thought you would've had problems with...you know."

"What are you talking about?" Ben asked as he pulled off the condom.

"You know. Coming."

"I did."

"I know. It just looked like you were having problem shooting your load."

"That's because my orgasms aren't all crotch sneezes."

Jason looked perplexed but didn't seem to want to admit he didn't know what his cousin was talking about. He went inside with the others.

Kimani, on the other hand, was dying to know what Ben meant. He'd had a rather mysterious look at the Joss House when she had brought up Taoism and sex. Was this somehow related?

"You better go get your breakfast," Ben told her. "I have some calls to make."

"Woof, woof, woof," she barked wryly.

He crouched down to meet her gaze. She was instantly drawn into the dark depths of his eyes.

Patting her head, he said, "I'll see that puppy gets a treat later."

What did he mean by a treat? She felt giddy at the prospect, then chastised herself for being so silly. She should be wary of treats from him. Like candy, his treats might look and taste good, but it wouldn't be good for her health.

Heading back into the cabin, she found Ryan enjoying her French toast at the table and Jake pouring cereal and milk into three bowls, which he set on the floor.

"Breakfast for piggie, puppy and pussy," he said.

Claire appeared to look around the bowls for a spoon.

Jake read her mind. "Animals don't have hands, remember? Eat up."

Lisa and Claire exchanged glances but went to the bowls of cereal. Dipping their heads down, they did their best to slurp up the cereal. Kimani decided she would rather go without food than obey Jake.

He narrowed his eyes at her as he folded his arms.

"You better eat up, bitch. That's all you're getting this morning. And nothing Benji boy says is going to change that because this is *my* cabin."

She only stared at him.

"Suit yourself," Jake said, kicking over her bowl and spilling the contents onto the floor. "Guess it's too late to change your mind."

While Lisa and Claire tried to eat without getting milk and cereal all over their faces—

not an easy feat—Kimani looked around for her pen. What had Ben done with it? It wasn't on the table or anywhere she would have expected him to place something that wasn't his. Had someone else taken it?

Jake had stepped away but he came back, holding a collar and what appeared to be a remote control. He crouched down beside Claire.

"Eat up, piggie," he said, pushing her nose into the cereal and milk. "Piggies are messy animals. Make sure you slurp it all up or you'll have to be a pet for the entire day. That means you'll have to piss outside when you need to go."

Derek, having thrown himself onto the sofa, watched a golf tournament on the television. "I think I'll skip skiing today. It's much more fun playing with the girls. What should we have them do next?"

"Mine isn't done being a piggie," Jake replied. After waiting for her to finish the last of her cereal, he said, "Mine didn't do so hot. She didn't go after the plum and she failed to swallow my load. So I've got a little something to motivate my little piggie. Sit up."

Claire sat on her knees. Milk glistened on the lower half of her face. Kimani tried to assess how the young woman was holding up and thought she saw apprehension in her crystal-blue eyes.

Jake snapped the collar around Claire's neck. "Let's test this baby out."

He turned a switch on the remote control.

"Oh, fuck!" she screamed, grabbing the collar as it shocked her.

"Piggies don't have hands," he reminded her. "That'll cost you."

"That hurts!" she cried when he shocked her again.

"You should turn the setting down," Kimani blurted, noticing the collar was set to seven out of ten.

Jake glared at her and pushed the button to shock Claire again. "You can thank your friend for that."

"Please, stop!" she sobbed, falling to the floor.

"Stop it!" Kimani exclaimed when she saw Jake about to press the button again.

"You don't learn either, do you?" Jake asked her. "Too bad I don't have a second collar for you."

He increased the shock intensity to an eight and pressed the button. Claire screamed and writhed on the floor.

"Mercy!" Kimani said for Claire.

"Dude," Jason said. "Maybe you should lighten up."

"Mercy, mercy!" Claire seconded.

"I know what I'm doing," Jake said. "Besides, she's *my* slut."

He turned the setting to nine, but before he could press the shock button, Kimani knocked it out of his hand.

Her voice trembled as she spoke. "She said 'stop.'"

"You fucking bitch," Jake spat. "Your friend's gonna pay for that."

He reached for the control, but Kimani dove for the same. He reached it first and shoved her to the ground. With a shake of the head, he turned the setting to its maximum.

Everyone stared at Jake, but it didn't seem to Kimani that anyone was going to stop him.

"What the fuck is going on?"

Ben! Kimani could have shouted with relief.

"You need to get your pet one of these," Jake said. "She's not very good at learning."

Ben walked over and looked down at Claire, who lay trembling on her side, sniffling and holding back her tears.

"Her face is wet," Ben noted.

"That's just milk from her cereal."

"It's dripping down her neck. With electroplay, it's best to keep things dry."

Bending down, Ben removed the collar from Claire. A muscle rippled along Jake's jaw.

"I wasn't going to play with it long," Jake explained.

Rising, Ben slowly scanned the room. He could probably sense the awkwardness.

"Did she say she was into electroplay?" Ben asked Jake.

"She said she was open to trying anything."

Ben turned to Claire. "Now that you've tried it, do you like it?"

Meekly, she shook her head.

Jake tossed Ben the remote control. "It's all yours then. Might be more effective on your pet anyway. She could use it."

He grinned at her. But she saw through his poise. He hated her now more than ever.

CHAPTER FIFTEEN

"I'd like to take the boat out," Ben said to Jake, who had plopped himself on a sofa near Derek.

"Keys are over there," Jake replied, waving at a console.

"Let's go," Ben said to Jason, when it looked like his cousin was going to sit down with Jake and Derek.

"Woof, woof?" Kimani asked.

"You're learning to ski, so you don't have to pretend to be a dog anymore."

She looked at Lisa. "Can we put something on?"

"Sure."

Jake shook his head. "Give 'em an inch..."

"I think we've had this conversation before. You worry about yours. I'll take care of mine."

Kimani was kneeling next to Claire, who had gotten to her knees. "Are you doing okay?"

Claire nodded.

"Do you want me to stay?"

Ben pressed his lips together. He hadn't given her a choice in the matter.

"I'm fine," Claire replied.

Kimani looked tentatively between Jake and Claire.

"Come on," Lisa urged Kimani. "I have two bathing suits, both brand-new. You can borrow one."

After Lisa and Kimani had left, Ben looked down at the collar and controller he held. Not trusting Jake enough to leave it behind, Ben decided to put it up in his room. He changed into his swim trunks and went downstairs. Claire sat on the floor next to Ryan by the dining table. Derek and Jake looked engrossed in watching the golf tournament.

"When I played the course, I made par on that hole," Derek said.

It was as if the women didn't exist.

Ben was looking forward to getting out on the lake without Jake or Derek. He had told Jake yesterday that he wanted a meeting with the other baller, but Jake had yet to set something up. Ben couldn't understand how the Whitehurst Sports Agency was so successful if that was how Jake ran things.

"I'm so glad I finally get to wear my bathing suit," Lisa said to Kimani after the women had returned from upstairs. She wore a tropical-print halter bikini with ties at the sides of the bottom.

When Ben turned to Kimani, he got hit with an instant boner.

Having spent the morning naked so far, the tiny bikini seemed to accent her assets *more*. Since the bikini was Lisa's, it was at least two sizes too small for Kimani. The shiny gold triangles barely covered half her tits, and the boyshort bottoms hugged her like a second skin. He could almost see the curves of her pussy lips.

"Nice swimsuit," Jason told Lisa, wrapping an arm around her waist.

Kimani gave Claire one last look before following the other three out onto the patio and down to the boat.

"I hope she's going to be okay," Kimani said.

"Jake's not going to really hurt her," Jason replied.

"You seriously believe that?"

"I've known Jake since we were freshmen

at college."

"He had the controller cranked up to its highest setting."

"He was just messin 'around."

"I don't think Claire appreciated his 'messin 'around,'" Kimani retorted with heat.

"She said she was okay," Lisa said.

Kimani didn't look convinced. She turned to him. "Do you think we can trust Jake?"

Ben started the engine, avoiding her penetrating her gaze. "I don't trust most people."

Not allowing him to eschew the question, she persisted. "Would you trust Jake not to hurt Claire?"

"Ben's only known Jake for two weeks," Jason said. "I've known him for years. He's never hurt anyone."

"How could you know for sure?"

"I was his roommate for all four years in college. I've seen him do just about everything."

"You thought he should tone it down with the shock collar. He didn't seem to listen, though."

"I don't think he heard me. He was too annoyed with *you* at the time."

"And he punished Claire for that!"

"You shouldn't have gotten in his way."

Ben cut them off. "That's enough."

He drove the boat to a calmer part of the lake.

"Claire is going to be fine," Lisa said to Kimani, who still looked unsettled. "She knew what she was getting into."

"Did she?" Kimani replied with doubt.

"She said she was curious about BDSM, and wanted to explore it with a guy who's super alpha."

"I'm not sure if he's super alpha. Super asshole, maybe."

Ben smiled to himself. It was pretty much his assessment of Jake.

He cut the engine.

"Try this one," he said, holding a lifejacket. She put her arms through the jacket and inhaled sharply when he cinched the vest over her chest. He found a pair of gloves for her, then checked the rope and its knot. He grabbed a pair of skis and waved for Kimani to go with him to the back of the boat, where he adjusted the skis before helping her into them.

Let's go," he told her before jumping into the water.

As expected for Northern California, even

in the summer, the water was on the cold side, but he welcomed how the coolness took him to a new level of wakefulness. Plus, it would help keep him from developing a hard-on whenever he glimpsed her arse.

"Toss the handlebar out," he told Jason. With the bar in one hand, he pulled Kimani to him with the other. He gave her the handlebar.

"Keep your knees to your chest with the skis pointed up," he instructed. "The boat's going to pull you up onto the skis."

He put his hands on her arms. "Keep your upper body strong. Hold tight to the handlebar."

Though he didn't have to, he wrapped his arms around her to keep her in position. He called to Jason, "Take the boat out nice and slow."

Turning back to Kimani, he said, "Try to keep those skis perpendicular to the surface of the water. And remember—strong upper body."

Once the boat had pulled the rope taut, he yelled, "Go!

Jason stepped on the accelerator, and the handlebar tore out of Kimani's hands.

"I'll hold on tighter next time," she said.

They swam to the handlebar. He helped her into position, wrapping his arms about her again. The coconut scent of her hair product filled his nose. He was tempted to roam his hands over her body, but that wasn't why they were out here. He yelled for Jason to start again.

This time the boat pulled her over the skis and into a face plant.

"You held on tighter," he praised.

She wiped the water from her eyes and coughed. "Yeah."

"It's like learning to ride a bicycle. Once it clicks, it'll be easy."

She grabbed the handlebar. "Let's go."

He smiled at her eagerness. Jason straightened out the rope, then hit the accelerator. The boat dragged her several yards, but she wasn't able to get up. Eventually the boat pulled the handlebar out of her hands. They tried several more times with varying results and two more face plants.

"We can take a break," he said, seeing that water had just splashed up her nose.

"Are you kidding me?" she returned.

Pleased with her determination, he presented her the handlebar. She gripped them and furrowed her brow in concentration. Jason stepped on the gas, and this time she got up. Ben could hear her squeal in delight. He watched her glide atop the water. The boat pulled her for several minutes until Jason turned it around to head back to him. The angle was too much for Kimani, whose skis slid out from beneath her. She went down. Jason stopped the boat and waited for Ben to reach them.

"That was awesome!" she shouted, her eyes gleaming. "Can we go again?"

Though he would have liked the excuse to put his arms around her again, he had a feeling she didn't need him anymore.

"As many times as you like," he answered as he climbed onto the back of the boat.

He watched her grab the handlebar, and the boat now easily pulled her out of the water. She stayed upright longer this time, going the entire length of the lake.

"You want a turn next?" he asked Lisa.

She shook her head. "I'm not really a sports person."

He took the steering wheel from Jason and decided to try some turns on Kimani. She was able to keep up till she crossed the wake from the first time and went down. He turned the boat around.

"Keep going?" he asked, looking down over the side of the boat at where she treaded water.

"You bet!"

She took a few more turns before finally coming in for a break.

"Can I get next?" Jason asked.

Ben nodded as he watched Kimani take off her gloves and vest. He liked the way her face glowed with excitement.

"That was so much fun!" she beamed as she took a seat near him. She surprised him with a mischievous smile, her manner more lighthearted than he had seen till now. Her voice lowered. "I like my treat. Thank you."

He returned her smile. "That wasn't your treat."

CHAPTER SIXTEEN

A flutter went through her. What kind of treat did he have in mind, then? *Stop it, Kimani. It doesn't matter. You're not here for that, remember?*

Her stomach rumbled, and she remembered she hadn't had breakfast.

"You want something to drink or eat?" she asked Ben, as if she hadn't heard what he had just said.

But by the look in his eyes, he knew that she had heard just fine. She found it difficult to swallow.

"I don't need anything," he replied. "At the moment."

Ignoring the latter half of his statement, she went to see what was in the cooler. Finding water and some pretzels, she went to join Lisa, who was sunbathing at the front of the boat.

"Isn't this the best?" Lisa asked. "I'm

gonna make four thousand dollars—maybe more—just lying on a boat."

"And playing fetch with a sadistic jerk," Kimani mumbled in between pretzels. She didn't see how Lisa and Ryan could remain fairly indifferent to all that Jake did. Most of all, she wondered about Claire. She could see the anxiety in the young woman's eyes. What if Jake turned out to be as bad as the guy who beat up Marissa?

"Where else are you going to make four thousand dollars in *one* week?" Lisa inquired.

"There are actually—"

"I mean someone like me. I don't have a college degree, and I sure as hell don't want to go back to working jobs like waitressing or painting nails."

"So you like how things are going so far?"

"I don't like having to sleep in a basement. I mean, I'm hanging out with rich guys, right? I kind of expected a little more, you know, luxury. But Jason's cute. I think he likes me, too."

"Have you felt uncomfortable at any time?"

"I could skip eating cereal from a bowl, but other than that..."

"If you were made to do something you

didn't want to do, would you feel comfortable enough to speak up?"

"Well, I'm not as adventurous as Claire. There were a number of things on the questionnaire we filled out that I ranked a one for 'not interested at all' for their one to five scale I don't think Claire put anything less than a three on all her answers."

"Did you get pressured into putting down higher numbers?"

"Some. I did change some of my answers from a one to a three."

Kimani made a mental note of that. To her, this was a pattern in the Scarlet Auction's behavior. "Why did you do that?"

"The woman administering the questionnaire said that I would get a higher bid if I was more open to things."

"Jake seems to be running the show here. Are you scared of him at all?"

"A little. I'm glad he's not my buyer, even if he is gorgeous. But a lot of women dig assholes. I mean, every romance I read has an alpha asshole for a hero."

Looking in the direction of the cabin at the far end of the lake, Kimani wondered what Claire and Ryan were doing at the moment. Hopefully nothing. Hopefully Jake wasn't taking his anger out on Claire.

Maybe she shouldn't have interfered with the shock collar. Maybe Jake wasn't the problem she saw him to be.

No. She trusted her instincts on this one. And it wasn't just because Jake had hit her. But how could she get Claire to see the darkness in Jake?

It's not your job to get her to see that. You're here to report on the story, not become involved in it.

"Too late for that," Kimani told herself, glancing over at Ben. How was she going to get herself out of this mess? What would Sam say?

With a moan, she put her head in her hands. She did not relish the idea of having to tell Sam everything. And he wanted more information on Ben, not less. A part of her regretted mentioning Ben. At the time, she *herself* had wanted more information on Ben. She hadn't trusted the guy and wanted reassurance that he wasn't some ex-con with a violent record or a dubious past.

It was still possible he was an ex-con. As for a dubious past, he had admitted to being part of a gang. So, she really hadn't gotten the assurance she sought at all. Instead, she'd complicated matters. She supposed Sam didn't have to know every part of the story—the part where she came undone at Ben's hands, let him tie her up, acted the part of his pet dog, and went down on him harder than she had ever—

"Are you okay?" Lisa asked.

Realizing she had groaned out loud, Kimani straightened. "I'm fine. I just...the whole collar thing with Claire still has me shaken a bit."

"Claire's going to be fine. Even if she's not a hundred percent happy at the moment, she will be when she gets that big fat check at the end. You should just chill and enjoy yourself. You're with one of the hottest guys in the world."

Kimani couldn't help but wince inwardly. "He had me bark like a dog."

"I'd bark like a dog for him and more. Hell, I'd kill to be his girlfriend. Do you know how much his family is worth?" Lisa looked Ben over. "Plus, he's a hunk *and* he gets you off. What more do you want in a guy?"

Kimani had had this conversation before, but she answered, "Kindness, integrity, intelligence, a sense of humor. You know, the 'boring' stuff."

"He might have all those things. And the best part is, he likes you."

Kimani stiffened. "I'm sure it's pretty easy to meet his standards for a sex toy as long as one is well-behaved."

"Maybe. But he looks at you a lot. And in *that way.*"

"What do you mean by 'that way?'"

"Sometimes it's just a hungry look, like he's a wolf and you're Red Riding Hood. But when you were skiing, it was...I don't know. Different."

She didn't know what Lisa was talking about, except for the hungry look. *That look* made her brain slow to a crawl. Lisa was probably just trying to make her feel better about her situation or take her mind off Claire. While she was eternally grateful to Ben for taking her off Jake's hands, she felt safer when she'd thought he might be more asshole than nice guy. If he was a nice guy, he wouldn't have made her crawl on all fours and blow him in front of the other guys. Right?

But it was in the context of sex play, so she shouldn't be too upset with him.

She reached for another pretzel and chanced to glance Ben's way. He was looking in her direction. And though he had his shades on, she recognized *that look.*

CHAPTER SEVENTEEN

"You want to go again?" Ben asked Kimani after he had skied and gotten back into the boat.

Her eyes lit up. "Sure!"

After taking off his lifejacket, he helped her into hers, trying not to stare at her tits as he did so. He helped her into the skis, then took the wheel from Jason, who went to join Lisa at the front of the boat.

"Wait." Ben grabbed him. "Make her come today."

Jason rolled his eyes. "You know that most women take *forever* to come?"

"Is she like most women?"

"I don't know."

"Then find out."

"I paid for her so I wouldn't *have* to worry about finding out."

Ben narrowed his eyes. "You're worried that you can't."

"It's a hassle, man."

"Just man up and do it."

Jason gave an exasperated sigh. "If you weren't my cuz..."

He went over to Lisa, who yelped when he shook the water from his hair over her. Ben couldn't understand how Jason didn't get the high from making a woman orgasm, watching her come unglued and knowing he had taken her there.

Even something as simple as watching Kimani ski, the water spraying behind her, knowing that she enjoyed herself and that he had facilitated her pleasure, was satisfying. He liked her athleticism and that she seemed to enjoy the physical challenge. Her initial setbacks with skiing hadn't daunted her, but seemed to have made her more determined to master the skill. He looked forward to seeing that same trait in the bedroom.

Bloody hell. He was growing hard again.

Kimani went for a solid twenty minutes before gesturing that she was done. He was ready, too. Lisa and Jason had started making out, and the thought of having Kimani kept taunting his mind.

Turning off the engine, he went to the stern to help her aboard. With ease, he hauled her out of the water and set her on the platform.

"I had no idea water-skiing could be so much fun," she said, sitting down as he began to help her with her skis. "I don't think I ever would have tried it if... Thanks for showing me."

"You're a natural," he said, taking her other foot from the ski. Their gazes met, and it was all he could do not to throw himself on top of her. He helped her to her feet to undo her lifejacket.

"I know how these work," she said, watching him release the first buckle.

"I know you know."

"I'm also not five years old. I could have taken the skis off myself, too."

He released the last buckle, slid the vest part way down her arms, and yanked her to him. He stared deep into her eyes. "I know that, too."

Her breath seemed caught in her throat. Her lips parted in that way that drove him wild.

She didn't look away, and her chin was tilted upward, making her mouth available for the taking. He had wanted to taste those full lips of her since he'd set eyes on them, wanted to feel their softness beneath a hard kiss. He could kiss her now. And he would.

But a squeal from Lisa pulled Kimani from the micro-world that had encased the two of them.

"I should get some water," Kimani said. "All that skiing worked up a thirst."

He kept her trapped in the life jacket and toyed with the idea of kissing her anyway. She could worry about her hydration later. Why was she resisting the moment anyway?

Lisa giggled, and Kimani tried to pull away.

He released her. She was just delaying the inevitable. He was going to have those lips, and waiting longer just meant he would be hungrier when he finally feasted.

She stumbled toward the cooler and pulled out a bottle of water. Ben glanced toward the bow, glad to see that Jason was still engaging in foreplay with Lisa. His cousin had his hand down her bikini bottom.

"So are we going to head back to the cabin now?" Kimani asked.

He looked at her. "Not before I fuck you in that swimsuit."

That lower lip dropped again. She gathered herself. "You don't mince words."

"Should I?"

"No. I appreciate it when you're straightforward."

"Do you?" He suspected his straightforwardness unsettled her.

"Yeah. Sometimes you give vague, mysterious statements that are hard to figure out."

"Like what?"

"Like leaving me no clue as to what was behind curtain number three or answering my questions with a question."

"You ask a lot of questions."

She stiffened. "Just making conversation, trying to get to know you better."

"Is that all?"

She furrowed her brow. "Doesn't it make sense that I would try to know you better?"

"We're not on a date."

"I know that," she replied quickly. "But since we're not fucking every single minute here, we might as well pass the time getting to know each other."

He sat on the side of the boat, opposite her so he had a full view of her. "I don't think it's wise to get to know each other too well."

"Why's that?"

"The only thing between us is sex. It

should stay that way."

She scrunched her face. "Are you worried I'm going to develop feelings for you?"

She had him taken aback this time.

"Ha," she huffed in bemusement and scorn. "Trust me, I don't want this to be anything more than sex either."

"Women have a tendency to complicate things," he explained, oddly perturbed that she seemed opposed to the idea of falling for him.

"That's a sexist generalization."

He crossed his arms. "You saying it's not true?"

"Even if it were true to some extent, I'm not that kind of woman. Like you, I'm not looking for a relationship. And if I were, I sure as hell wouldn't be looking for it through the Scarlet Auction."

She had said as much their first day, and he believed her. It was part of the reason he was willing to buy her. She wasn't starstruck like the other women. But just to be sure, he decided to play devil's advocate.

"So where would you look for a relationship?"

"No particular place, but if I had to name something, church would be a better place than the Scarlet Auction."

"So why *aren't* you looking for a relationship?"

"Why aren't you?"

"No answering questions with questions."

She pursed her lips. "Like I said before, I'm busy. Is that so unusual?"

"The others are interested in relationships."

"How can you tell?" She grinned as an idea came to her. "Let me guess: men have a special radar that signals if an approaching woman is looking for a relationship. A warning alarm goes off in your head so you can avoid her like she's some heat-seeking missile."

"Something like that."

"So what does your radar say about me?"

She leaned forward, unconsciously creating more cleavage. Blood rushed to the area of his groin. Warning signals were going off, but for a different reason.

"I believe you. You're not looking for a relationship," he answered.

Satisfied, she sat back. "Maybe I'll think differently when the ticking of the biological clock gets louder, but for now, a relationship would be a distraction. I need to focus on my career."

He eyed her carefully. "What career is that?"

She faltered. "Well, um, I know I don't want to be working as an office assistant for the rest of my life."

"What do you want to do instead?"

She took a sip of her water before replying, "I'm open to different things."

"Such as?"

"I thought we weren't supposed to get to know each other too well?"

"I thought you liked making conversation." He stood up. "Or would you rather be doing something else?"

Silence fell between them, but that meant they could both hear Lisa cooing and Jason grumbling something with the words "hot" and "inside you."

"Is...is it treat time?" she asked, pulling up her legs in a self-protective manner.

He advanced toward her. "Or 'make-up' time."

Puzzled, she raised her brows.

"You said you were going to make it up to me," he explained.

"I did," she acknowledged, possibly regretting what she had said.

Too bad for her.

"You have something in mind?" she asked.

"I do."

"What does the 'make-up' involve?"

"Penetration."

Her lashes fluttered as she looked down. She glanced up at him. "I could give you another blow job."

He paused. Did she think she was going to get away with not having a cock in her pussy? He leaned toward her till mere inches separated their faces. "We could make it hard and rough sex, the way you like it."

"I like what?"

"You rated it highly on your questionnaire. ."

She swallowed audibly. "You saw my questionnaire?"

"Were you lying?"

"I—not exactly, but..."

"You also had a five down for sex without a condom."

"I changed my mind."

He cupped the side of her face and ran his thumb along her plump bottom lip. "I hope you were being honest with the rest of the questionnaire. I don't like lies."

Her gaze dipped down.

He grabbed her wrists and pulled them together in front of her. The water bottle clattered to the floor.

"You promised to be good today, and if there's one thing I dislike more than lies, it's broken promises."

Her breath grew even more uneven as he leaned in closer."Wasn't I a good pet for you this morning? More than metaphorically?"

She didn't sound too happy referring to the earlier events.

"You made a very good puppy," he acknowledged as he pulled her to her feet.

"You have a thing for animals?"

He swiveled the chair around and bent her over the back of it. "You're the one who put down a five for role-playing"

He held her in place with a hand on her mid-back and looked down. *Holy shit.* He lifted his shades to the top of his head to better marvel at the fine piece of ass presented to him.

She ignored his point. "Do you get a rush from degrading women?"

He fisted his hand in her hair and yanked her head up, making her gasp. He had to be careful, though, with her fine hair. He put his mouth near her ear. "You accusing me of something?"

"Depends on your answer."

"Is that how you felt? Degraded?"

"Yes. How would *you* feel if you had to crawl on all fours and bark like a dog?"

He reached beneath her to feel her up. "Degraded and humiliated."

Bollocks. He had been curious to see how far Kimani would go, but he shouldn't have let Jake get away with his little farm animal scene.

"So how come you still like what I do to you?" he asked her, pressing his pelvis into her and relishing the feel of his cock on her backside.

"Some of what you've done has been okay."

He ground himself into her as he continued to massage her tits. "Just 'okay?' I think you like it all more than you're willing to admit."

And to prove it, he moved one hand down between her legs to find a part of her bikini was wetter than the rest. "That there tells me all I need to know."

He rubbed his fingers against her, making her whimper. The area of his groin tightened. God, he wanted to fuck her so bloody badly. With one hand he groped a breast while he fondled her with his other.

From the bow of the boat came the sounds of Lisa panting and Jason grunting.

Ben turned his focus back on Kimani. "You want my cock inside you, don't you?"

Lust was searing through his veins, and he shoved his hips into her a little harder than he intended.

"Yes..."

He yanked down the boyshorts, revealing her two perfectly shaped spheres. He sank his fingers into the suppleness of one, then gave it a light slap. Releasing her buttocks, he reached a hand around her waist. The bikini bottom still clung tightly to her hips, but he forced his fingers beneath the fabric to find her clit. Since she was supposed to be just a fucktoy, he could've taken her without regard to her arousal. But he wanted to annihilate any lingering resistance. He stroked her with slow and languid caresses till she moaned for more.

With more patience than he thought he had, he fondled her till she gushed with wetness. He knew he was hitting the right spot when she remained stiff and unmoving, as if worried that the slightest shift would result in a deceleration of pleasure. Her breaths and gasps were erratic yet constant, building in intensity as her climax drew closer and closer.

But he wasn't going to let her off that easily.

"Are you ready to be fucked?"

She didn't respond. He slid his fingers along her slit, toying with the entry.

"Are you?" he asked.

"Are, um, you sure you don't want another blowjob?"

She shivered when he worked a breast with his other hand.

"But we don't have a condom," she demurred.

"You think I wouldn't have thought of that?" he murmured into her ear. He licked her earlobe, kissed the back of her ear, and sealed his lips to her neck. She gave a surrendering groan. He plied her clit, dug his hand into her breast, and sucked her neck, working her into a frenzy.

When it seemed she was approaching her orgasm, he slowed all stimulation. He repeated his question, "Are you ready to be fucked?"

She mumbled something intelligible.

He withdrew his hand from between her thighs. "Was that a 'yes'?"

"Yes."

It was a meek admission. He could have been nice and left it at that, but he wanted her unequivocal consent.

"How badly do you want my cock?"

She drew in a ragged breath. "Very badly."

"Bad enough to beg for it?"

He reached into the pocket of his trunks for a condom. But he waited for her answer before he did anything else.

"Please, please give me your cock."

"Where do you want it?"

There was a pause before she answered, "In my pussy."

"You sure? You sure you don't want it in your mouth?"

She moaned, then murmured, "My pussy, please."

He ripped open the condom, pulled out his cock, and slipped the condom on. Pushing the bikini out of the way, he slid his erection beneath her to that inviting, moist heat. He pressed his tip against her slit.

"I like how you beg."

When he didn't move, she got the message. "Please, please give me your cock."

"What do you want it for?"

"I want you to fuck me."

That undid him. He grasped her hips and guided his shaft into her.

"Oh, Jesus," she mumbled when he had sunk an inch inside.

He shut his eyes. *Fucking marvelous.*

Her skin, cool to the touch when he had pulled her from the lake, had warmed but was nowhere as hot as the furnace wrapped about the head of his cock. He pushed himself farther, stretching her slit.

"Ahhh..." she groaned.

"Beg if you want more."

She drew in a deep breath. "Um...please..."

"Please, what?"

"Please, may I have more?"

He smiled because her question came out with a slight accent, as if she channeled Oliver Twist.

"More what?"

"More cock," she mumbled.

He pulled her up on her toes for a better angle before pushing himself deeper. He wanted nothing more than to let loose, shove his entire length into her, and pound her to kingdom come. But she felt tight. Like she hadn't had sex in a while. So he decided to take it easier on her. He reached for her clit again as his cock throbbed madly, wanting to be fully buried inside of her.

Her pussy flexed against him as his fingers hit all the right spots on her swollen pleasure bud. Desire flooded him with the potency of narcotics, but better than narcotics because arousal invigorated.

"Ready for more?" he asked.

"Yes," she murmured.

He pressed several more inches into her. She gave a faint wail, then started to breathe as if she were going into labor.

"Oh, Jesus," she pleaded as she adjusted to the thickness inside her.

Ben had to take a long breath to contain himself. He usually didn't feel the sensation to climax this early. Focusing on her clit helped. It was nice and engorged, and he knew the spot that made her legs tremble. Her moans signified her growing pleasure. Soon she wouldn't care about any discomfort stemming from his cock filling her.

"Oh God, oh God," she panted.

He eased more of himself in. Her pussy

flexed about his cock, sending currents to the tips of his toes. The contractions increased as he agitated his digits against her. Slowly, he withdrew his cock.

The motion sent her over the edge as she dissolved into minor convulsions, crying out as she spasmed against his hand, the chair, and his pelvis.

He thrust into her sweet wet heat, spearing himself into her as deeply as he could. He pulled his hand out of her bikini, grabbed her hips, and began seeking his own end. He bucked against her, his pelvis slapping into her arse. She was so wet, so hot down there. She grabbed the edge of the seat to keep from flying over the back of the chair.

It didn't take long to reach his orgasm. His body jerked against her, his ab muscles contracted, but he slowed in time to keep the ejaculation at bay. When the climax faded, he pulled his still-hardened cock from her. A final shudder shook him from head to toe.

But he was ready for round two.

CHAPTER EIGHTEEN

Kimani was glad when he came because getting drilled into the chair by his hard body was getting more than uncomfortable. But when she turned to him, she saw that his cock was still erect. Very erect.

How had he not come? She had felt him shaking against her and heard his roar. As with the fellatio earlier, he'd had all the signs of climaxing.

Ben whipped the bikini bottom off, swiveled the chair back around and pushed her into it, spreading her legs open with his. Stepping back, he surveyed her. Hunger flamed in his eyes, and when his gaze fell to her pussy, bared for him, a grin tugged the corners of his mouth. Till yesterday, she had never felt so intimately exposed. But today was even worse. With her legs spread, her pussy angled up for him, her position was much raunchier. And she was outside. With Lisa and Jason a few yards away.

"This is a pretty good way of making it up," Ben said.

Leaning down, he braced himself against the chair with one arm while his other hand traced her clit with the tip of his cock. A breeze cooled the wetness coating her private parts. The haze of her earlier orgasm hadn't yet dissipated, and she wasn't sure what to make of it all. The touch of his cock to her clit felt unmistakably good. He rubbed his shaft along that traitorous bud. He might as well own her clit. All it did for her was muddle her thinking and make her give in to urges she should be resisting.

Okay, it also gave her some sweet, sweet orgasms. But she didn't like the feeling that she wasn't in charge, wasn't in control.

He dug his cock into the spot that made her want to crawl out of her skin with glee. She moaned. It was awkward and hot all at the same time. *Just go with it*, her desires whispered. Besides, she didn't want to upset him and then have to make it up to him again. He might not give her his cell to call Sam. And she didn't like broken promises either. She would make good on her word.

So she didn't budge when he pointed his cock at the entry below her clit. It had been a while since she'd had sex, and she had felt every millimeter of him when he had pushed into her. At first, it hadn't felt great, but the pleasure he elicited from her clit overrode the discomfort, and gradually she had begun to enjoy the sensation of being filled by him. She loved penetration from the backside. Doggy style was her favorite. Especially when combined with clit play.

She was a little worried about her current position, though. He'd angled her up, and with her pussy pushed up toward him, he could go deeper.

He sank the crown of his cock into her, pulled out and rubbed her clit, then sank back in. He repeated this several times, till she wanted to scream for him to plunge more of himself into her.

Wait. Was that what she really wanted?

Hovering over her, he filled her space. She could feel the warmth of his body and hear his every breath. She saw nothing but him, his unblemished skin, the veins in his neck, the glisten of sweat upon his chest. The height of the chair did not make it easy for him. It was too high for him to kneel, too low for him to stand. And given her position, he would have to do most of the work. But she didn't doubt his endurance.

He nestled his cock an inch or two farther, grunting, "God, your pussy feels so good."

Your cock feels so good.

He was back to sliding his shaft along her clit. The muscles below contracted at the loss. As good as his attention to her clit felt, she found herself wanting to feel his hardness inside her.

Adjusting his stance, he pushed his cock back inside her. With small motions, he thrust his hips, hitting the bundle of nerves behind her clit. She screamed as her body warred with itself once more, wanting to stretch out while wanting to remain still at the same time. When he came out, she wasn't sure whether she was disappointed or relieved. He toyed with her clit some more before reentering.

Oh Jesus, oh Jesus.

She couldn't take this level of pleasure. So blissful. So torturous. He withdrew again. Was he taunting her or giving her breaks? Against her will, she whimpered.

"Do you want more?"

She stared wide-eyed into the depths of his dark irises.

Hell, yes!

But the more cautious part of her, now a more timid voice, suggested it was better and safer not to go there. She'd had an orgasm already. Was she really ready to take on another?

She didn't have much of a choice. Ben pushed into her. He hadn't gone even half the length of his cock. She started grunting as his cock pistoned in and out. She felt the urge to pee blooming.

No.

Yes...

No!

Yes!

He didn't withdraw this time but kept a steady rhythm. She screamed again as rapture exploded. When he pulled out, a spray of wetness followed. He plunged back in, a little farther this time, sending more waves of pleasure through her body. Another mist of wetness followed as he came out. He rubbed his cock all over her clit before diving back in.

"That's the way to come for me."

She was still riding the high of her orgasm

when he started pumping himself into her deeper and deeper. He elicited more wetness, till her whole lower body, her pelvis, her belly, the backs of her thighs were covered in fluid.

She screamed and cursed when he buried himself to the hilt this time. He pulled the triangles of her bikini top aside and groped a breast as he quickened his pumping. Sweat fell from his forehead onto her. Despite being overwhelmed with sensation, she couldn't take her eyes off of him. He met her stare, sending bolts of arousal into her.

She could feel another climax building. He drew out his thrusting and rested his forehead against hers, locking her gaze with his. She gave an agonized cry as her body erupted once more.

O.M.G.

He shoved himself into her and bucked his pelvis furiously inside until he came, grunting and shaking. The throb of his cock stretched her. He *had* to have come. She hoped he had, because she wasn't sure she could keep going. Several tremors went through him before he finally pulled out of her and stood. His legs had to have been sore, but he made sure to help her get comfortable before stretching himself out.

As her sense came back, she realized how loud she'd been, and that she was covered in her own juices, and his sweat. Flushing, she wondered how best to clean up after herself.

He eyed the chair as well. "Looks like we found something else you're a natural at."

Her blush deepened.

He grasped her jaw and tilted her head up. "You like that?"

"Thank you for my treat."

He smiled. "That wasn't your treat either."

CHAPTER NINETEEN

Bright and large, her eyes were so compelling, it was hard to look away. The way she'd looked up at him from the chair, her lips plump from her biting them when she'd been holding back, as he sank into her sweet wetness, had sent him hurtling toward an ejaculating orgasm. He hadn't even bothered trying to fit in an extra climax.

"Oh," she said in response, looking rattled and maybe a little alarmed at what he had said.

He released her jaw and took off the condom, wondering if he would get to feel her pussy without a barrier in between before their week was over. Tossing the condom in the wastebasket, he looked over at Jason and Lisa, both of whom had dozed off, with Lisa curled into Jason's arm. Ben couldn't be sure, but he suspected his cousin had met the challenge of getting Lisa off.

"We should go back to the cabin and check on the others," Kimani said as Ben handed her a bottle of water to replenish the fluids she had lost through squirting.

He didn't want to go back to the cabin and would have preferred taking a dip in the lake or ski again. But he could see she was concerned about Claire, so he pulled on his swim trunks and started the engine.

Kimani fixed her top and found a towel to wipe herself. He watched her wiggle into the bikini bottom, which wasn't easy given that her skin was moist, before starting to steer the boat toward the cabin. He almost asked how she was, and why she was so concerned about Claire, but let it go. Too much about her distracted him.

She wiped down the chair next. He smiled to himself. Women and cleanliness. His older sister, Phyllis, was a fanatic about it. Her boyfriend once complained that she wouldn't have sex unless the bedroom was completely straightened.

"So, um," Kimani began, looking pensive, "it almost seemed like you came more than once. Did you?"

"You mean just now?"

She nodded.

"I came twice."

"What about this morning when I was blowing you?"

"I think I came four times."

Her eyes widened. "Really? How is that possible?"

"You didn't know that men could have multiple orgasms?"

"No. What about the refractory period?"

"You only need a refractory period if you ejaculate."

"You can have an orgasm without ejaculating?"

"It doesn't come naturally, but you can train yourself. The retention of semen is one of the foundational tenets of Taoist sexual practice."

"Oh. Are role-playing and tying a girl up part of Taoist sexual practices, too?"

"No. I do those just for fun."

"Do you normally engage in a lot of kinky stuff?"

"Sometimes. When I feel inspired." He'd been having fun exploring Kimani's limits, what she liked, and what she didn't, what made her angry, and what made her flush with arousal.

She didn't say anything after that, and he

was glad not to go down a path that would lead to him getting aroused again.

When they got back to the cabin, they found Claire and Ryan on top of the coffee table on all fours. Jake was pounding Ryan from behind, and Derek did the same with Claire. Claire didn't look like she was enjoying it as much as Ryan.

Looking up, Jake said, "Our pets made sandwiches for you guys."

They looked over at the dining table, which had several plates of messily put-together sandwiches.

"They don't look all that great because, you know, they're not allowed to use their paws. You should've seen them try to scoop mayonnaise out of the jar."

"I don't care," Jason responded, walking over to the table. "I'm starving."

"Time to switch," Jake said to Derek.

They exchanged positions and resumed fucking the women.

"Squeal for me, piggie," Jake said to Claire. "Show daddy how much you like it."

Claire gave a high-pitched squeal. It was followed by an unplanned cry when Jake thrust himself hard into her.

"Who fucks you better?" Jake asked. "Me

or Derek?"

"You, sir," she murmured.

"Piggies don't talk, remember?"

"Oink, oink."

Jake laughed. "Time to switch again."

They changed places again.

"So he fucks you better, eh?" Derek asked Claire as he pounded viciously into her.

"You want to join us?" Jake asked. "It's my version of speed dating: speed fucking."

Ben turned to Kimani, who was looking around as if she had lost something. "Go get something to eat."

She and Lisa went to join Jason at the table.

"You're missing out," said Derek.

"I've got a call to make," Ben explained.

A call had come in from his uncle about the same time he was making Kimani into a fountain. He went upstairs to his bedroom to change out of his swim trunks and call Uncle Gordon back.

"I'm sorry to disturb you while you're on vacation," his uncle apologized. "But Dawson Chang got pretty upset with me, and I thought maybe you could help smooth things over."

Dawson was the head of the Asian Pacific

Community Alliance, or APCA, a group that wielded significant influence on any developments in or near Chinatown.

"Why was he upset with you?" Ben asked as he sat down.

"I told him that I didn't have anything to do with my brother's company or his development projects, but Dawson is convinced otherwise. He has a number of things he wants out of the project, and he can't see himself backing my candidacy if he doesn't get them."

Ben pulled out the pen he had absentmindedly put in his pocket and began to fiddle with it. "That sounds like extortion."

"It's just politics. He doesn't need to have a specific reason to endorse or not endorse me."

"Are you sure you want to set a precedent?"

Uncle Gordon sighed. "I didn't promise him anything. I just said that I'm sure you would want to sit down with him anyway."

Ben was aware that no project made it through City Hall if it met with strong resistance from the APCA, but he hadn't planned on sitting down with Dawson until after the election.

"He wants to meet this week," Uncle Gordon added. "He has a trip planned for Taiwan and will be out of country for three weeks. I'd rather not wait that long to get his endorsement."

Ben spun the pen over the top of his hand. He *had* wanted to get Kimani out of here for awhile...

"I'll meet with him this week," he said.

"Thank you, and I'm sorry you're having to cut short your vacation. How are you liking—where are you again?"

"Trinity County."

"Oh. Is it nice up there?"

Recalling how sexy Kimani looked bent over the back of the chair, he replied, "It's nice."

"I'll let you work out the meeting details yourself with Dawson. I think it's best I'm not at the meeting. I don't want to reinforce any idea that I'm involved with your projects. Do you have Dawson's phone number?"

"I have it somewhere, but if you have it on hand, I'll write it down."

He fished a receipt out of the wastebasket and clicked the pen.

Nothing happened.

He clicked it twice, but the ballpoint still

didn't protrude.

"...7589," Uncle Gordon finished.

"Actually, just text me the number."

"Will do. Thanks again, Ben."

After hanging up, Ben unscrewed the pen to see how it was jammed.

It wasn't an ordinary pen, he discovered. Aside from being thicker than usual, it had a USB inside. Did the pen double as a jump drive? Reassembling the pen, he got it to work and put it back in his pocket.

"I can meet tomorrow morning, say nine o'clock," Dawson said when Ben called him.

"How about a breakfast meeting at eight-thirty?" Ben suggested.

"Okay, I can make that work."

Hanging up, Ben considered leaving Jason and the unprotected women alone with Jake and Derek. But Jason was an adult, and he wasn't his cousin's keeper. He wasn't anyone's keeper. Except for Kimani.

Reasoning that he could always return the same day if needed, Ben called his pilot, who was staying in Weaverville, to have the jet ready and arrange for the car rental to pick up the Jeep at the airport. He then started to pack. The shock collar and remote were on the dresser. Deciding not to leave it in the cabin with Jake, who clearly was all talk and no real knowledge, he scooped them up and dropped them into his suitcase.

"We'll take good care of your pet for you," Jake said after Ben had gone downstairs to announce he would have to return to the Bay Area for a meeting the next day.

No chance, Ben replied silently, noting Kimani's alarm. Aloud, he said, "I'm taking her with."

He instructed her to change and get her things. She got up from her chair but started scanning the rug around her.

"What's the matter?" he asked.

"Nothing," she replied. "I was just seeing if I accidentally dropped my pen around here."

CHAPTER TWENTY

"Get your things," Ben told her. She should jump at the chance to get away from the cabin, away from Jake, but Kimani hesitated. What about Claire? What about her story? Even though she would have a chance to talk with Ben alone, he wasn't her story, despite Sam's interest in him. The more she focused on Ben, the more she would have to explain her own role in things. But did she dare stay without Ben's protection? Surely that wouldn't be wise.

Ben stared at her. "What are you waiting for? Go get your things."

She bristled at his commanding tone. He raised a brow. At that, she turned to head downstairs. This was the part of this week she liked the least—being told what to do. And being treated like a child about to be grounded when she didn't hop to.

The massages and silk ties were cool,

though. So was coming. And squirting.

She shivered at the memory, her body warming at the prospect. Jesus. It was like she was getting addicted.

She still couldn't get over the fact that he could orgasm without ejaculating. That a guy could stay harder longer ought to be exciting news. But in her case, it was scary.

It didn't take long for her to throw all her things into her handbag and a plastic shopping bag. She braided her hair and changed into the long skirt, glad to be out of Lisa's tiny bikini.

"When are you coming back?" Jason was asking Ben when Kimani got back upstairs.

As she entered the room, she pretended to adjust her shoes as she slipped another of her recording pens into the potted palm.

"I'll let you know," Ben answered, his suitcase beside him.

"Bring Slut #2 back in one piece," Jake said from where he sat on the couch with a shot of bourbon.

"Like I said before: you worry about yours, I'll take care of mine."

"Well, she's really mine, too."

"You sold her to me."

"I see it more as a loan. I'm renting her

out to you."

Ben frowned. "Two hundred thousand dollars is a purchase price, not a borrowing price."

"Yeah, but it's my signature on the auction documents."

Lisa whispered to Kimani, "You're so lucky. I bet you won't have to sleep in a basement tonight."

"He could have something worse than a basement," Kimani whispered back. She turned to Claire, who apparently had a reprieve from pretending to be a pig and was sitting at the table playing with the ends of her hair.

"You doing okay?" Kimani asked.

"Yeah," Claire said.

Her answer sounded a little hollow to Kimani. At least she wouldn't be completely alone. Ryan seemed to have backbone, and maybe the two other guys would step up if Jake got out of hand.

Maybe.

"You know you're allowed to speak up if you don't like something?"

Claire nodded.

"Ben—I mean, my buyer—was nice enough to let me borrow his cell. Maybe one of the other guys would do that, too, if you needed to make call."

"Who would I call?"

"You could call me—on Ben's phone."

"Enough chit-chatting," Jake barked.

The Scarlet Auction should have provided the women a means of aid, Kimani thought angrily. But it was increasingly apparent that the Auction did everything to handicap the women.

She and Ben spent the first half of the drive to the Weaverville airport in relative quiet. Ben seemed preoccupied, and she kept trying to assuage her guilt about leaving Claire by thinking through all the ways Claire could get help. She had her safety word, but would Jake honor it? Kimani had planted the idea of using a cellphone. Jason seemed the nicest of the other guys. Maybe he would let Claire use his.

"Are we flying back after your meeting?" she asked Ben.

He glanced at her. "Are you eager to return to the cabin?"

"Yes and no."

"Is it because of Claire?"

She wondered if she should be forthcoming. Could she truly trust Ben with the truth? He didn't seem to like Jake, but some men adhered to the "bros before hos" mantra and circled the wagons if they felt a woman was attacking one of their own. But she had to take that chance. She had to find an ally. Either way, she'd learn what kind of man he was.

"I don't trust Jake," she said. "He's an asshole."

"He gave you that bruise, didn't he?"

She touched her cheek. The hue had started to recede a little today. "Yeah."

Ben was looking ahead at the road, so she couldn't quite make out his expression.

"You're not Claire's keeper," he said. "She's a full-grown adult, not a child—"

"She's barely an adult. I don't think she's old enough to drink. Definitely not old enough to rent a car."

"You're barely old enough to rent a car free and clear."

"My point is that I don't think Claire is experienced enough to handle herself in a tough situation. And I *am* her keeper."

"How are you her keeper? Did you know her before the Scarlet Auction?"

"I'm her keeper because I'm a fellow human being. It's the right thing to do, to care about the well-being of others."

"That's a big undertaking, to be the keeper of everyone else."

"I didn't mean it that way."

"You have a right to live your own life."

"But if I have the chance to help someone out, it wouldn't be right to be purely self-serving."

"You don't know that Claire is going to need your help."

"I wish I *could* know."

She thought about the recording pen. It had a battery life of twelve hours, so it basically would only cover the rest of the day until they all went to bed. And it certainly wouldn't prevent anything. It would only capture the audio of whatever transpired.

"I'll check in about Claire," Ben offered.

"How?"

"I'll talk to Jason."

"Your cousin seems pretty loyal to his buddy."

"Family commands more loyalty. Jason's the younger brother I never had."

"Was he in your gang, too?"

"He was one of the reasons I didn't fight my dad when he sent me to boarding school. Jason was interested in joining, and my dad said it was because I was a bad influence."

Placated, Kimani settled into her seat and watched the scenery go by. "I should thank you for buying me from Jake. Claire seems to tolerate him, but I'd rather blow a donkey than that guy."

Ben's lips curled. "You like him that much?"

She suddenly regretted her words. What if he made her do something with Jake to punish her? She wouldn't do it. Turning to Ben, she said, "And don't even think about making me touch that jerk—for any reason."

He raised a brow at her. "You think you get to decide what happens?"

He wouldn't. Would he? To make it clear, she said, "I'm adding an item to my big turn-offs: giving head to racist assholes."

Ben laughed. "All right. I'm not ready to share you yet anyway."

She stiffened. "Share?"

"You put a five down next to gangbangs. Or don't you remember?"

Shit. That damn questionnaire. She had no idea it would come back to haunt her.

Because I'm not supposed to be having sex with anyone!

"That—I wasn't thinking of getting banged

by a bunch of jerks."

"What kind of men do you think the Scarlet Auction attracts? Kind and caring gentlemen?"

She pursed her lips. She couldn't tell him the real reason she had put 5's next to everything on that questionnaire. And she was pretty much prejudiced against every man who participated in the Scarlet Auction. Although Ben hadn't been there the night of the auction, by buying her, he was an extension of the Auction audience.

"Are you saying you're not a kind and caring gentleman?" she challenged.

"You said I was an asshole."

"Not the kind of asshole that Jake is."

"I don't have a problem with being an asshole."

"Do you like it better than being a gentleman?"

"I like being me. A lot of men you think are gentlemen, are actually assholes."

She had to agree with that. Was it possible that assholes could then turn out to be gentlemen? Probably not.

She decided to change the subject before he recalled other things she might have said or done that she wished she could redo. "So what kind of meeting do you have?"

"A work meeting."

"About a development project?"

"Yes."

"Which one?"

He gave her a sidelong glance. "Are you just making conversation?"

"It beats sitting in silence."

"It's a waterfront property in Oakland."

"Mixed use?"

"That's the intent."

Sam had wanted her to look into Ben and the mayoral race, but she wasn't sure what he expected her to find.

"You haven't decided what you're going to build?" she asked.

"We have a proposal, but usually there's a lot of negotiation that happens before anything is finalized. The city wants to see certain things, community groups want things. It can drag the process out."

"I bet having a family member in the mayor's office will help move things along?"

"It could, but it's not automatic. There are a lot of governing bodies involved, such as the Planning Commission. And my uncle's not the kind of person to greenlight a project just because he's related to the developer. My uncle has never had anything to do with my father's business."

"You said family commands loyalty."

That seemed to give Ben pause. Would his uncle choose loyalty or integrity?

"Do you know your uncle well?" she asked.

"Growing up, I know he didn't want to have anything to do with money. My father tried to recruit him into the family business. Uncle Gordon wanted to be a penniless lawyer instead."

"A penniless lawyer?"

"He wanted to be a civil rights attorney. He represented immigrants and tenants in housing projects. People who couldn't pay him. When my father offered to take care of his law school loans, Uncle Gordon got mad."

"Sounds like a cool guy."

Ben smiled. "Not the words my father used."

"I can see how your uncle could be perceived as ungrateful for not accepting such an offer."

"My father called him a spoiled idiot."

"That's harsh. Is that what you think of your uncle?"

"Nothing's absolute. I thought it was

short-sighted not to accept the offer to have his student loans wiped out, but if I thought he was an idiot, I wouldn't be supporting him for mayor."

"No? He *is* family. Doesn't that command loyalty?"

He appeared to be in thought, then said again, "Nothing's absolute."

"Not even family?"

"Not even family."

They continued the rest of the ride, quiet in their own thoughts. Ben's pilot greeted him at the airport and gave a friendly acknowledgment to Kimani. He didn't ask any questions and Ben offered no explanations, which made her wonder if he often had random women accompanying him on flights.

The Embraer Legacy jet had room for twelve passengers. Four of the leather seats circled a gleaming wooden table. The elegant sofa next to the bar could seat at least three people, and the rest were reclining leather armchairs.

Kimani marveled at the plush carpeting beneath her feet. She had never been inside a private jet before.

"Sit anywhere you like," Ben said. "I've got

to take care of some work."

He situated himself with his laptop at the table. Taking a seat beside a window, Kimani went through the available magazines, some of them in Chinese. She settled on *The Economist.*

After reading an article about how worldwide universal health care was within reach, she looked out the window at the farmland below. The closer they got to the Bay Area, the more she felt at ease. She would be close to her apartment and Marissa, family and friends, and Sam.

Remembering that she had yet to call him, she went to Ben and inquired, "Have I qualified to use your cell again?"

Her defenses went up in case he decided to move the goalposts, but he pulled out his phone and handed it to her.

"Thank you," she said as she went into the bathroom.

With its artisan sink, fancy fixtures, and a shower, the bathroom was as nice as any found in a luxury hotel. Admiring the pot of orchids on the counter, she idly wondered if Ben took care of watering the flowers himself, but surely that was too mundane for a billionaire. Then again, Ben was unlike anyone she knew.

"I was starting to get worried," Sam said shortly after picking up.

"I'm actually headed into the city," she explained. "Ben had a meeting come up."

"Really? What kind of meeting?"

"A meeting about their waterfront development, but how is that related to the Scarlet Auction?"

"It doesn't, but a good journalist is open to any story, right? So far, nothing that interesting is happening in the Oakland mayor's race. You have a unique opportunity here."

She bit her bottom lip. *I guess...*

"I would like nothing more than to have you work at the *Tribune*," Sam added. "There's an ownership meeting in two months. If we can end this quarter strong, hopefully they won't think to talk exit strategies."

"You think they would shut down the paper?"

"In this day and age, that's always a possibility with traditional print. By the way, why did Lee decide to bring you along?"

Because I'm his fucktoy.

Aloud, she said, "I think he's bored and

just wanted some company."

"Has he made you do anything—you know, for him?"

She was saved from having to answer right away by a text that came in.

"What was that?" Sam asked.

"A text came in from some Rosenstein guy," she replied absentmindedly as she tried to come up with a suitable answer to Sam's previous question.

"Rosenstein the developer?"

"I don't know."

"What does the text say?"

"Wouldn't that be an invasion of privacy?"

"We're not using this as incriminating evidence of anything. I'm just curious if it's Ezra Rosenstein, one of the biggest developers in the state."

"It just says 'Half a million in commits for the PAC already.'"

"Hm."

"I need you to find out what you can about Jake Whitehurst," she said. "I've got a bad feeling about him."

"He's the guy working with Ben on some sports deal?"

"Yeah."

"Will do. If you're in the city, do you think

you'd be able to swing by the *Tribune* office tomorrow?"

"I'll try."

She didn't mention that she would have to get Ben's permission first, but she was relieved that Sam seemed to have forgotten his earlier question.

After she exited the bathroom and returned to her seat, Ben came to sit down next to her, handing her a mug of tea as he took his phone back. It was green tea, but she didn't mind it as much this time. Maybe she was acquiring a taste for it.

He watched the landscape pass by with her before saying, "I want to specifically thank you for keeping me from going off on that CHP officer. It wouldn't have helped Uncle Gordon if I'd created a stir of any kind."

She was tempted to point out that "buying" a woman for sex would be much more scandalous than a brush with law enforcement.

"Every time I see a cop, I think of Sandra Bland," she sighed.

"Who's that?"

"A twenty-eight-year-old African-American woman who died in jail three days after she was arrested for a traffic stop. Her story is one of many in the #SayHerName movement. Police brutality on black men can make it into the news, but what happens to black women is often invisible. It's similar with the Asian-American community, right? Because Asian-Americans aren't seen as a historically repressed race, even though the Chinese are the only ethnic group ever to be banned from the country by an act of Congress. It's just better if we protest racial injustice in public forums."

"That's not necessarily safer."

Thinking about the man who had driven a car into a crowd of counter-protesters in Charlottesville, killing a young woman, she had no rebuttal.

"Still, it probably wouldn't have gone well for either of us if I had said what I really wanted to say to that wanker," Ben acknowledged.

"When I was growing up, my parents always made sure I acted differently in public places so as not to draw attention. Don't talk as much. Don't laugh too loud."

"But you grew up in the Bay Area, didn't you?"

"The Bay Area is more progressive than most other places, but there's still prejudice.

My uncle was a hairstylist at a popular beauty salon. When women found out he was black, some rescheduled their appointments. He was good, though. In fact, he's better with white people hair than he is with black people hair. He once tried weaves on me. It did *not* turn out."

She perked up at the thought she just had. "Would I have time to make a visit to my stylist? My hair could use some attention."

He looked over her current braids. "I like the pigtails."

"I'm feeling microbraids."

He frowned. "That could take hours."

"You seem like you have a lot of work to do. You don't want to have to babysit me."

He took that into consideration before responding. "If you want to take the time to get braids, you may not have time for sleep...because I have a lot planned for you, pet."

CHAPTER TWENTY-ONE

After the jet had landed, Ben didn't get up right away, though Kimani jumped from her seat with eagerness. She gave him a quizzical look.

"I'm expecting someone to meet me on the jet," he explained.

She sat back down, and he was surprised she didn't pounce to ask who it would be. The hatch opened, and a minute later a nurse boarded.

"Mr. Lee," she greeted, setting down her medical tote and unpacking supplies for a blood test. She handed him a form.

He nodded toward Kimani. "Results should be sent to her."

The nurse gave Kimani the form instead. He presented his arm to the nurse, who began to feel for a vein.

Kimani looked over the form. "STD test results?"

"Just put your email address down as the

recipient," he instructed. When she looked up at him for more information, he explained, "You were worried that I didn't go through the usual Auction protocols."

The test wasn't just to ease her fears. He wanted to ditch the condoms.

"I see," Kimani said as she put down her email address. "But…"

She waited for the nurse to be done drawing blood.

"How long before the results come in?" he asked the nurse.

"Twenty-four hours is the fastest the lab can process the samples," replied the nurse, "but we will endeavor to get you results as soon as possible."

She taped a bandage on his arm, packed the vials into a plastic bag marked "STAT" and added the form Kimani had filled out.

"Even if the test results came back negative for anything," Kimani said after the nurse had left, "safe sex is still good practice if we don't want to end up with anything unexpected."

"Didn't the Scarlet Auction administer birth control shots to all the participating women?" he asked.

"They did. Jake tell you that?"

"I was forwarded the information."

The thought of sinking into her sans a condom made him consider fucking her in his jet, but Bataar, his security detail, entered. Bataar, who would have received the intel on Kimani from Stephens, was unsurprised to see her.

"Bataar is my head of security," Ben introduced.

Kimani, who seemed in a more carefree disposition since landing, gave the large Mongolian a friendly smile. Though he knew Bataar would be greeting him, he wasn't particularly happy to see the man. He didn't want anyone intruding on his time with Kimani.

"How was Trinity County?" Bataar asked. "I'm still disappointed you didn't have me come. I've never been to that part of California."

"Nothing was going to happen to me there."

"You never know. And it's not where you are as much as who is there."

"You already did a background check on everyone."

Kimani piped up. "Did he do a background check on Jake Whitehurst?"

Bataar raised his thick dark brows.

"He's nothing to worry about," Ben assured.

"I don't know about that," she grumbled. "It wouldn't surprise me if he tortured defenseless animals as a kid."

"What makes you say that?" Bataar asked her.

"I can handle Jake," Ben said as much to her as Bataar, whom he told, "You can follow me if you want tonight, but I don't want to know it."

Bataar glanced knowingly between him and Kimani. "You got it, boss."

After deboarding, they were met by his driver, Wong, and the GMC Yukon. Wong was a small man but he liked his cars large. Kimani seemed lighter on her feet. When Wong opened the car door for her, she got in almost cheerfully.

Being away from the cabin was good for her, Ben decided. He got in the back of the car with her.

"Can we get something to eat?" she asked as her stomach rumbled. "I just realized I've pretty much only had pretzels the whole day."

"What happened to breakfast and lunch?" Ben asked.

"I didn't want to eat Jake's breakfast, and the sandwiches were soggy."

He directed Wong to head into Chinatown.

"Do you live here in the city?" she asked as they drove up Highway 101.

"I have a place in Pacific Heights. How about you?"

"I share a flat with my roommate, Marissa, in the Haight. Marissa's the one who...first told me about the Scarlet Auction."

"Was she a participant, too?"

"I'm not supposed to say."

"The nondisclosure agreement you signed says you're not supposed to talk about your week in any detail, including where you went and who you've met."

She didn't meet his gaze when she answered, "I know."

"But you've already told your friend Sam."

"I only told her I was going to be away for a week having sex."

"I'd say that's pretty descriptive of your week."

"I haven't told Sam anything else."

That was an outright lie, but he didn't call her on it for the time being.

"Do you spend most of your time here in the city?" she inquired, clearly wanting to change the subject.

"Lately I've been traveling a lot, but I do like San Francisco. It reminds me of Chongqing."

"I wish I could visit China someday."

He found he would like to take her there. It was not a welcome sentiment. He was only supposed to care about the sex when it came to Kimani.

"Where is your meeting tomorrow?"

"In Oakland at the Pacific Room."

"That's a nice place. Must be an important meeting."

"It is. Are you just making conversation again?"

She scowled at him. If she did that again, he was going to yank her over to him and shove his hand up her skirt.

"You like to make things difficult," she said.

"You want conversation. How about I ask the questions?"

As he expected, she didn't look too thrilled about that. She replied, "Go ahead, as long as I get to be as difficult as you about them."

"So what did you do after graduating Stanford?"

"I went home and lived with my parents to save money while I looked for a job"

"What kind of a job?"

"I ended up doing an internship."

"What kind of internship?"

"It was with a local paper out in the East Bay."

"You're interested in journalism."

"It's pretty interesting. Now do I get to ask some questions?"

"I wasn't done."

She frowned. "I thought it was best we didn't get to know each other too well."

"I think I'm changing my mind about that."

"Oh. We're not supposed to talk too much about ourselves. I'm sure I read that somewhere in the Scarlet Auction guidelines."

"Are you worried I'm going to find out something about you that you don't want me to know?"

"Yeah. We're supposed to go our separate ways when this is all said and done. How do I know you're not going to try to stalk me afterwards?"

"Maybe I should worry about the same."

"Don't worry. I'll be as done with you as you are with me at the end of the week."

She turned her attention to the windows, a possible indication that she was done conversing. He let her be since he needed to look through his emails. They had four more days before they were done with each other. Four days didn't seem like a long time.

He called his cousin to see what they, and especially Jake, were doing. Jason replied that everyone was chilling and watching a movie. Jake didn't seem interested in doing anything and had spent the last hour on his laptop.

"So he hasn't done anything to Claire?" Kimani asked, having overhead his conversation.

"Not so far."

"Day's not over," she said with a furrowed brow.

Wong drove up the main drag in Chinatown, lined with businesses and teeming with people jostling their way past displays of fruits and vegetables and trinkets for tourists. Turning off Grant Avenue, Wong stopped in front of a small restaurant.

"Food," Ben announced.

He led Kimani inside the hole-in-the-wall that had somehow crammed six tables in a space meant for two. The server greeted him in Cantonese and gestured for them to seat themselves. Good Chinese restaurants often came with what Westerners would consider poor service. Ben ordered bowls of noodle soup and green tea. She didn't complain about his choice in beverage.

"Oh my God, this is so good," she gushed after taking her first bite of noodles.

"That's because they're hand pulled and freshly made each morning."

She scarfed the noodles down, along with the beef broth garnished with green onions, and even drank four small cupfuls of tea.

After dinner, they walked past a butcher shop where roasted ducks and pigs hung in the windows, to a bakery, where he bought her a coconut custard bun.

"I can pay you back as soon as I get my wallet back," she said as they took a seat on a park bench in Jackson Square.

"You think I'm going to worry about the ten dollars I spent on your noodles and dessert?"

"No, but it's the responsible and hospitable thing for me to do, to pay you back. This isn't a date, after all."

It wasn't, but somehow it felt like one. But better than a date because they had gotten the sex out of the way.

It was dark when they got back to his penthouse.

"Nice place," she murmured as she took in recessed ceiling lights gleaming off the wood floors and the twenty-foot-tall floor-to-ceiling windows, which offered a panoramic view of twinkling house lights with the bay as backdrop.

Turning her head, she gasped. "You have a basketball court!"

He had converted part of the patio space to a small court and installed a regulation basketball goal.

"Can I check it out?" she asked.

He nodded before dismissing Wong, whom he wouldn't need for the rest of the evening. When he joined her outside, she had found a ball and was dribbling. She pulled up in front of the basket and knocked it down. She retrieved the ball and went for a layup next.

"This is one sweet setup," she said after he had turned on the porch lights for her.

She turned around, dribbled, and pulled

up for a jump shot. He admired her form and her explosiveness. She had the fast-twitch muscles necessary for a good basketball player.

Despite wearing jeans and his Adidas slide sandals, he made a move and stole the ball from her. He hit his own jump shot.

She put her hand on her hips. "Was that a challenge?"

He raised his brows. "You want to go one-on-one?"

She looked down at her long skirt and, pulling it up, created two knots on either side so that the skirt stayed above her knees. "Let's do this."

He bounced the ball to her to start. She took a little rock step and drove to the basket for a layup before he was ready to properly defend her.

"You're quick," he acknowledged. "Like Steph Curry."

She grinned and threw him the ball. "Let's see what you've got."

Given their height difference, he could have simply shot the ball over her, but he made it interesting for her, dribbling it one way, pivoting, and driving down the baseline. He had to come to a stop to make his shot, but that was when she made her move and stole the ball. She swung to the other side but missed her shot. He got the rebound and a dunk.

He could see her competitive drive amp up. Her eyes sparkled. Her next move involved a hesitation step and a crossover. Her smaller size and quickness gave her the edge as she dribbled by him for a successful layup.

In the cool night air, they went for several turns each at the basket till they were both sweating and breathing hard. She was up a basket when he caught his own rebound and threw the ball back up in a fade-away jumper. When he came down, however, he stepped into her, knocking them both toward the ground. He managed to twist himself beneath her so she would land on top of him instead of the other way around. Her chest slammed into his. She shook off the rattle of the fall from her head and met his gaze.

Before she could catch her breath, he cupped the back of her head and crushed her mouth down to his.

Fucking glorious.

He had been waiting for this moment, and her lips were every bit as sweet as he had imagined they would be. He ravaged her mouth. Selfishly. Greedily. Her surprised gasps were muffled by his ferocity. He devoured her lips till they were bruised and swollen before delving into her mouth and tasting the wet heat there.

She eventually managed to catch up and kissed him back. Pleased, he allowed her to take over some of the action and welcomed her tongue into his mouth.

The area of his groin, seeking to release the tension gathered there, thrust into her pelvis. With his free hand, he grabbed her hip and ground her into him. The knots in her skirt had come undone, and the voluminous garment fell over them. She managed to straddle him, and press herself down on his hardened cock, making his head swim with the prospect of her riding atop him. She wanted this. And knowing that was intoxicating.

He bucked his hips at her while he continued to brutalize her mouth. If he didn't have such a raging hard-on, he could spend hours sucking her lips and working every inch of her orifice. He nestled a hand beneath her skirt and caressed the smooth, bare skin of her leg. He dropped the other hand to the back of her neck, one of his favorite places.

After several minutes, they were both breathless. Cupping the back of her head again, he turned her to the side and brought his lips to her ear. "I think it's time you got your treat."

CHAPTER TWENTY-TWO

Though her lips were sore, Kimani did not relish the interruption in action. Her body was on fire. It craved him, and nothing could satisfy her lust except Ben.

In one movement, he managed to roll her off him and pull her onto her feet as he got up. Taking her by the hand, he led her back inside and to the door of what was perhaps a bedroom. He opened the door and turned the dimmer switch to low. The chandeliers above cast just enough light for her to see everything.

A large bed took up part of the room. Windows displayed the skyline, and a sitting area nestled nearby. She could see into a bathroom with a Jacuzzi tub and walk-in shower. Erotic art decorated the walls.

"The painted handscrolls are replicas of famous shunga," he explained, noticing her gaze. "It's a Japanese term for erotic art."

The scrolls featured couples in various

poses, their kimonos and robes entwined about their half-naked bodies.

On another wall were photographs. In the first one she saw, a woman wearing a kimono was bound neck to foot in rope.

"This one is from the bakushi Chimuo Nureki," he explained. "I had the chance to see him live in New York once before he passed away."

He pointed to the second photograph of a woman dangling upside down in rope suspension.

"Naka Akira is very well known in the world of erotic rope bondage."

Surprisingly, she could see why he liked this form of art. In addition to the highly erotic qualities, there was something elegant about the rope bondage.

Recalling how he had tied her with the neckties, she ventured to ask, "You ever do anything like that?"

He raised a brow. "You interested?"

"I was just curious."

"Well, if you change your mind, yes, I can do rope bondage."

Her breath left her. She wondered what it would be like to be bound like that? Heat rose in her as part of her became titillated by the thought of being tied up by Ben. She wondered what else he could do?

Without a word, Ben stepped in front of her, gripped the scooped neckline of her tank top and began tearing it down the middle.

Hey, I paid for that. Or, I will have once I've paid you back.

Letting the ripped garment dangle from her shoulders, he shoved her sports bra above her breasts. The tight band of the bra pushed down on the orbs. Standing in front of her, he slid his hand between her thighs. "I like how wet you get for me."

She moaned as he found all the right spots.

He smiled. "You like that, love?"

She nodded and involuntarily whimpered.

His ministrations sent flutters of pleasure through her loins. Whether fast or slow, hard or soft, his fondling drew her closer and closer to her climax. She could feel it pressing down into her clit, ready to explode.

"Show me how badly you want to come."

He stopped his fingers but kept them at her flesh. She did her best to grind herself into his hand, trying to rub her clit against the padded part of his palm.

"That's it, pet...I know you want to come badly."

With a groan, she pumped herself harder against him. With a small scream, she achieved the end she sought. She trembled against Ben till the last waves of rapture dissipated.

While she was recovering, he palmed a breast and massaged it. He tugged at the nipple and pinched it to hardness. After playing with the other nipple, he went to the dresser. "How many orgasms do you think can you give me?" he asked as he played with the other nipple.

"In a row?" she responded.

"In a row."

"I'm not sure. Three, four?"

He raised his brows. "Just three or four?"

"How many were you thinking?"

"Ten."

She did a double take. No way. Even if that were possible, she wasn't sure she'd want to come that many times.

He pulled out a cordless Magic Wand. She owned one of those herself, though not as large and high-powered as the one he held. He turned it on to its lowest setting and touched it to the side of her breast. The vibration startled her. He moved the wand closer toward the nipple.

Please don't touch my nipple.

He touched the wand to her nipple.

She shrank away from the vibration against her sensitive nub, but she couldn't escape. He touched the vibrator to her other nipple. She squealed and panted.

Lord, have mercy.

Mercifully, Ben moved the Magic Wand down between her legs. She breathed a huge sigh of relief. The wand tickled the hair at her pubis, its vibration sending beautiful caresses to her clit. It didn't take long for her arousal to build toward a second orgasm

"If you want to come, ask."

"May I come, please?" she asked.

But he knew what she intended and pressed the wand farther into her clit, adjusting the strength of the vibration higher. Her second climax erupted, making her legs weak as she writhed and twisted.

Flooded in bliss, she was ready for him to pull the wand away, but he didn't.

"I think we can rip another one out of

you."

What?! Get that thing away from me, she wanted to shout. Her clitoris was too sensitized to take any more stimulation. She scooted toward the bed, trying to move away from the vibration, but he jammed it harder into her. She shook her head and screamed.

"Breathe through it."

But she could only manage to pant furiously. Didn't he know she couldn't take any more?

Fuuuuck.

Then, to her surprise, her body found another plateau. The vibrations were still unbearable, but through the discomfort, the seeds of another orgasm managed to sprout.

Meeting his gaze, she drew strength from him. The third orgasm came on strong, obliterating the previous one. She thrashed against him as her climax wreaked havoc on her body. It was amazing. And intense. And amazing.

"Three down. Seven to go."

CHAPTER TWENTY-THREE

She looked so fucking gorgeous, trembling from her orgasm.

Ben had to take a few deep breaths of his own.

Turning off the wand, he set it aside. Too much vibration and her clit would go numb. Which was why he would use the Womanizer next. It stimulated through suction. With the new toy in hand, he turned her so her backside brushed against him, groped a breast and rolled it beneath his hand.

"We're just getting warmed up," he whispered beside her ear.

He ran his hand down her midsection and glanced at the mirror on the opposite wall. She noticed the mirror then. Together they observed her reflection, the rise and fall of her chest, the glisten of her wetness on her inner thighs. He curled his fingers into the patch of curls at the base of her pelvis.

"You know how fucking hot you look?" he growled, groping her in various places before grabbing her crotch.

Her breathing grew uneven.

"Especially when you come?" he added. He loved the way her brow furrowed and her eyes rolled toward the back of her head as she neared her climax. He loved that anguished look of awe when her body hit euphoria.

He parted her folds and fit the mouth of the Womanizer on her clit. He turned it on its lowest setting. Her eyes closed, and her moans sounded like purrs.

"I see you like this."

It didn't take Kimani long to start squirming. Her head fell back against him, pleasure clearly etched on her face. He turned the stimulation up to its next setting, engulfing her in waves of pleasure again. His cock throbbed angrily as he watched her chest heave. She looked dazed but still present. Her body quivered. She was close to coming.

"Oh my God," she wailed as her climax came. "Okay, okay!" she screamed after a minute. "Get that thing off me!"

He turned it off. She groaned after the suction released her clit.

"Did that make for a good treat?" he asked.

She shivered. "Oh, wow."

"One more orgasm before halftime."

"I don't know..."

He reached around her hip and brushed his fingers along her clit. She gave a violent shudder.

"I don't think my clit can take much more," she whispered.

"Which is why I'm going to finger-fuck you."

He sank two fingers into her pussy. Holy shit. It was a furnace in there. And drenching with her juices. He curled his fingers inside her.

"Really, I..."

"We're not stopping until you hit ten."

He stroked her gradually, feeling for the spot that would send tremors through her. Her moan was long and drawn. Every sound she made, every breath she took, sent currents to his cock. He'd have to fuck her soon, but first he was going to get her off one more time.

"Oh, Jeeeesus..."

She tilted her pelvis to give him a better angle. He quickened his pace a little, not wanting to rush things, enjoying the buildup of her arousal. Her hands searched for something to hold onto.

"Oh geez, oh God!"

He increased the pressure of his fingers and his rhythm. "Don't come yet."

She grunted.

He agitated his fingers intensely into her snatch. "Not yet."

"But—"

"Not yet."

"I can't—"

"Now."

Her eyes rolled as the orgasm shook her body. He withdrew his fingers, releasing a stream of fluid onto the floor. He shoved back inside her and pulled out more of her wetness. "Oh my God, oh my God," she grumbled in between hiccups. She sat down on the bed.

He had never made a woman hiccup before. Walking over to the mini-fridge, he got a sports drink. She would need the electrolytes along with the hydration if she was going to last five more orgasms.

Twisting the cap off, he handed her the bottle. She hiccupped, then drank readily. After several long gulps, she stopped to see if the hiccups were gone. They were.

"You did good," he said before taking a drink from the same bottle. "You're halfway there."

"Have you—have you actually made someone come this much before?" she asked in disbelief.

"I've done seven before, but not ten."

"Thanks," she replied wryly. "I feel so special."

He cupped her chin. "You *are* special, pet."

His choice of words surprised them both, and he dropped her chin and stepped away before they thought too much on it. He offered her more of the drink. She took several more sips.

After finishing the drink, he tossed the bottle into the wastebasket and surveyed her. "You squirted on my floor."

"Who's fault is that?" she retorted.

He smiled at her before pulling off his shirt. Her breath seemed to catch. He kicked off his shoes.

"What's next?" she asked.

He pulled off his jeans and then his boxer briefs, freeing his cock from the unwanted confines. "You always want to know what to expect. Ever go with the flow? Remember: I'm in control."

Naked, he stood before her. Her lashes fluttered at his nearness.

"Is halftime over already?" she asked.

"Time to start the second half," he affirmed.

He gripped her jaw. He was going to have himself another taste of those lips. This time he kissed her gently, savoring their lush softness. They had felt fucking unbelievable wrapped around his cock, and they were just as marvelous beneath his own. She gave herself into the kiss, returning the pressure, the sweep of the tongue, the nipping and sucking. When he pulled back, he saw the embers of desire still burned in her eyes.

She lay back while he put on a condom. He nudged her legs apart and slid his cock in between her thighs. He rubbed his length against her pussy lips. Back and forth. Back and forth. Collecting her wetness on his cock. He made sure to graze her clit, which had recovered from the Womanizer.

"Feel good?" he asked.

"Mmmm," she answered.

He angled his cock up at her slit and pushed in. She grunted.

"Tell me if you want more."

"More, please."

He pushed in deeper. She flexed about him, sending ripples of pleasure through his lower body. His toes curled.

"How about now?" he inquired.

She took several breaths before saying, "More, please."

This time he shoved all of himself in. Her eyes widened.

"Fuck," she gasped in surprise.

He withdrew. Then buried himself. Her pussy contracted again.

So bloody good.

If he had to spend the rest of his life buried inside her, his cock would have no complaints.

He grabbed the back of her thighs and lifted her so he could spear more of himself into her. He rolled his hips, making sure to find an angle that worked for her. At first, he varied the rhythm and the force of his thrusts to keep her guessing. She responded to them all.

He returned to thrusting in earnest. They moved their way up the bed with the force of their fucking.

"Oh God, yes!" she grunted.

After several minutes, she cried out, "Oh, *yes!*"

She contracted against his cock, and her limbs jerked of their own accord. He could barely wait for her orgasm to be over before he started drilling himself into her.

Fuck.

He couldn't stop himself from slamming her into the headboard. She was too bloody exquisite. Before he had time to catch himself, he blew his load. Digging his hold into her thighs, he shoved himself deep as the paroxysms took over, uncoiling all the tension gathered in his loins through his cock.

Fuck. Now he would have that refractory period. At least with Kimani, he was sure he could get it up again sooner rather than later.

However, she looked like she could use a small rest. After taking off the condom and tossing it into the trash, he selected a box of Ben Wa balls. He pulled out two silver balls attached to a string.

"Spread 'em," he instructed.

She was sitting on the bed with her legs bent. He nudged her knees apart and got a nice view of her snatch.

"Lean back."

She rested on her elbows. "Are those Kegel balls?"

"The original, you might say."

He brushed a ball along her sodden slit before pushing it inside her. He inserted the second one, then grabbed the wand again. Turning it on, he placed it over her slit. Her eyes lit up.

"Jesus, that feels *good*."

The Ben Wa balls were hollow and contained small weights inside. They were probably vibrating nicely inside of her. He slid the wand up to her clit. Closing her eyes, she lay back.

"Oh, *yes*."

He took in her every movement, her every sound as she soaked in the pleasure. He took her hands and placed them over her breasts. She squeezed and kneaded the orbs. As he expected would happen, his own lust grew quickly.

"Oh..."

"I like how wanton you get."

She moaned.

"Answer me."

"Yes."

He rubbed the vibrator over her. She gripped the edges of the sheets and started to writhe. As she climaxed, he felt himself harden again. Pushing her to her limits was fun and hot as hell, but there was something else about her that made him want to do everything to her.

After all her shuddering had dissipated, she lay with her eyes closed without stirring an inch. She looked as if she could stop right now and go to sleep.

Too bad. Like it or not, she was going to hit ten orgasms.

CHAPTER TWENTY-FOUR

Kimani settled into the bed with a contented sigh. She had made it to seven orgasms. She had never had that many in one day, let alone one session. But the last three would probably be the hardest. Her head was ringing from all the stimulation, and the rest of her was satiated. She really didn't want to get herself agitated again.

But he turned her over. She felt the balls move inside of her.

"I'm good with seven. Honestly," she said.

"You put me in charge," he reminded her. He sank his hand into a buttock and massaged it. "Try to keep the balls in."

She clenched her pelvic muscles as best she could, wishing she had taken up Kegel exercises. She felt him behind her, between her legs, and heard the rip of foil. Then she felt his cock pressing into her folds. With all the wetness there, he slid in easily. She still gasped when he filled her. His thrusts were slow and shallow at first.

"God, your arse is fucking lush," he said.

His voice made her muscles contract about his shaft. He sank deeper. She was desperate for an orgasm to wash away her lingering doubts. Her pussy grasped at him to spur him on.

He gave her derriere a light slap, then drove his shaft farther into her. If her legs weren't so tired, she would have met his thrusts. But she could offer little resistance, so every time he pushed into her, he shoved her into the bed. There was no give and take, no partnership. Her role was to be the receptacle of his spearing.

Except for the contractions of her vaginal muscles, which increased as he continued his pleasurable motions. She took solace in the little she could control.

Until he thrust a little too forcefully, smacking his pelvis into her. He kept a steady and faster rhythm. If it weren't for the fact that she wanted her orgasm badly, it might have been a little too much for her.

The warm and scintillating waves from her pussy were now stronger. She was close to coming.

"Come on my command," he said.

Come on command? How was she going to...

She felt her lower body quaking from the eminent climax.

"Hold it," he told her.

"Aargh, I don't think I can—"

"Yes, you can."

Then stop fucking me!

She tried her best to hold back the tide. It wasn't easy when she wanted to drown. "Hold it..."

She grit her teeth. *I don't want to hold it.*

"Now. Come for me."

But the convulsions had started before he spoke. In the moment, she didn't care. She knew only relief from releasing the euphoria. She almost cried in happiness. It felt so damn good. So damn good.

CHAPTER TWENTY-FIVE

She didn't quite make it to his command, but Ben decided it was close enough. He drove himself into her, relishing the sound of his pelvis slapping into her arse. Holding on to her hips, he thrust himself into an orgasm but kept from ejaculating because she still had two orgasms to go. After his abdominal muscles had stopped contracting, and the bliss of his climax had traveled through and out his body, he disengaged from her.

With her eyes closed, she lay limp upon the bed, looking spent.

"Two more."

"Oh, I don't know..." she murmured. "I'm not sure..."

Flipping her onto her back again, he reached over to where he had placed another toy, the LELO SONA. After fitting the nozzle over her clit, he chose a gentle wave setting and selected the lowest intensity. The SONA purred to life, sending sonic pulses into her. She stared at it, transfixed.

"What does it feel like?" he asked.

"Like a tide ebbing and flowing through my clit. Only...it's expanding. It's not just my clit."

Her eyes closed and her head dropped back onto his shoulder. He held the toy in place for several minutes as he watched the pleasure wave over her face. He turned up the intensity and her eyes flew open.

"Too much, too much," she gasped.

He lowered it back down. Within a minute, she was gasping, "I'm going to come!"

Almost immediately, she became a shaking mess.

"Jesus! Jesus!" she grimaced. She grasped the arm holding the SONA and squeezed him tight.

But just when he began to think it was time to turn off the device, she screamed and quaked more violently. She had hit the true peak of her orgasm.

When he finally powered off the SONA, shivers were still going through her, and her breath was completely erratic. She slumped against him.

"Holy shit..." she murmured.

He hadn't yet tried the SONA on anyone before but clearly it was a keeper.

"One more," he said.

She groaned. He could tell she was tired. But he wanted an even number. "You've got one more in you."

Feebly, she shook her head. "I don't know…"

He pulled her to the edge of the bed till her legs dangled toward the floor. "You're going to at least try."

"Okay, okay."

After putting on another condom, he stood at the side of the bed and settled between her legs. He pulled her toward him and impaled himself into her. She grunted but otherwise appeared half comatose. He slapped a breast to rouse her.

"No faking an orgasm," he warned. "Squirting is required on this one."

Her mouth fell open. She had to attend her body's desire now. He rubbed her clit with his thumb while he thrust nice and easy into her. Thirty minutes passed before she started moaning in earnest, but he could tell she was still a ways from coming. He reached for the SONA again.

"I don't know about that," she said.

"Shhh."

He put it over her clit and turned it on while he continued to buck his hips at her. Within minutes, her pussy started contracting wildly against his cock. It felt so bloody marvelous, he just might come before her, even without increasing the force or speed of his thrusting.

"Squirt for me, Kimani."

She started thrashing like a maniac. He had to hold her down with his free hand so she wouldn't buck off his cock until he was ready to pull out. When he did, fluid gushed from her, spraying his belly and his groin.

"G-Get it off," she said through chattering teeth.

He turned off the SONA, set it aside, grabbed her legs, and speared himself into her again. Over and over. Harder and harder. Till his orgasm bowled through him, a tsunami of pleasure.

Fuck.

He rocked backward. Her pussy was magnificent. *She* was magnificent.

Though she looked ready to fall asleep, he made her sit up and drink some water. He settled her into the silk sheets. He went to brush his teeth and splash cold water on his face. He had just extracted ten orgasms out of her in one session, yet he was already thinking about how to wrest ten more out of her.

When he returned, Kimani was asleep. Envious of the pillow she snuggled into, he pulled the covers back and lay down beside her.

It had been a good day. The water-skiing, dinner in Chinatown, the one-on-one, and of course the sex. God, the sex.

In her sleep, she rolled over. He moved his arm up, and her head landed in the crook. He wrapped his arm about her. This felt good, too.

Too good.

His mobile buzzed, indicating a text message had come in. He reached over to the bedside table to see who had texted. It was Jake.

> Need to call in my loaner. Turns out I'm not supposed to sell my purchases to third parties. You'll have to bring her back.

Coming up next...
HIS TO TORMENT

Excerpt
HIS TO TORMENT

CHAPTER ONE

What have I done?

Kimani Taylor had slept deep and dreamless, waking alone to the feel of luxury surrounding her body in the form of silken sheets and a feather bed.

Morning light streamed through floor-to-ceiling windows. Last night she had been too exhausted to appreciate the modern elegance of the bedroom that included a panoramic view of San Francisco's Pacific Heights, plush rugs over gleaming hardwood floors, and a gas fireplace six feet wide opposite the bed.

A part of her wanted to stay snuggled in the bed, but she had work to do. Too many times, thanks to one Benjamin Lee and his killer caresses, she had lost sight of her objective: to expose the Scarlet Auction and its exploitation of the women participating in its program. In doing so, she would become the journalist she was meant to be.

No more messing around with Ben. She wasn't here for sex. Or to be someone's sex toy. Besides, Ben had given—or maybe *extracted* was a better term—enough orgasms to last the week.

But he expected sex. If she wanted to get her

scoop and put a stop to the dubious operations of the Scarlet Auction, how was she going to accomplish that without having sex?

Deciding that the answer might come to her in the course of the day, she looked around the room for clothes but remembered she had left her things on a sofa in the main room, and Ben had torn the tank top she had worn yesterday.

A shiver went through her as memories of his touch played in her mind, making the warmth churn below her belly.

To quell the sensations, she wrapped a sheet around her nakedness and got out of bed. A clock on the wall indicated it was a few minutes past six. She opened the bedroom door and made her way into the living area.

Ben was outside on the basketball court going through what looked like *tai chi* movements. He wore only sweatpants, and she tried her best not to salivate at the sight of his sleek muscles. They had just the right amount of contour and hardness to them, not too puffy or swollen-looking. Most of the time, he had her too worked up to touch him. She imagined what it would feel like to run her hands over his pecs, his abdomen, his—

As if sensing her gaze on him, Ben turned around. His expression seemed to soften before he came inside. She decided that she liked the look of morning stubble about his jaw.

"Did you sleep well?" he asked.

She nodded. "Beats sleeping on the mattress in Jake's basement."

More like the bed was in an entirely different stratosphere.

His gaze took in the bedsheet she wore, and even though he had seen her fully naked, she couldn't help but blush. It was the intensity of his stare. That wolf-eying-red-riding-hood look.

Remembering her resolve to keep focused, she said, "I thought I would get in a shower before getting dressed, if that's okay with you."

"Sure."

"Thanks." She grabbed her things.

"You won't need the clothes from the thrift shop," he said as he headed into the open kitchen.

Was he going to make her walk around naked the whole time, like Jake required of the other women still at the lakeside cabin? She frowned at the thought, even though she had been plenty naked in front of Ben already. "Why not?"

Opening the black stainless refrigerator, he pulled out eggs and cracked a few into a glass.

"Aren't you afraid of getting salmonella?" she asked as she watched him down the raw eggs.

"The eggs are delivered fresh from a farm in Sonoma County. Their chickens are pasture-raised. The chances of salmonella are low."

"I've heard of cage-free eggs, but what's pasture-raised?"

"Cage-free doesn't always mean the chickens

get to roam in the fresh outdoors. They could still be in a cage, only it's barn-sized. And they could still be fed a corn and soy diet."

"Is that bad?"

"Chickens are omnivores. Like many other birds, they eat bugs."

"Oh. That makes sense, though I never thought of chickens that way. Guess I'll think twice next time I buy eggs with the labels 'cage-free' and 'vegetarian-fed.'"

She tucked the information away. There was a lot about the food industry that could make for compelling stories.

"So how do eggs taste raw?" she asked.

"Best way to find out is to try for yourself."

"You don't like them cooked?"

He cracked an egg into a new glass. "I like them cooked but there are certain benefits in their raw state."

He presented her the glass. She stared into it. The yolk stared back.

"Yogurt and granola is more my thing for breakfast…"

She wondered if he was going to make her drink the raw egg the way he made her drink green tea. To beat him to the punch, she downed the egg. She set the glass down as if she had just thrown back a shot of whiskey.

"That went down so fast, did you get a chance to taste anything?" he asked.

"Not really, but I don't think I'm missing out."

She saw a grin tug a corner of his mouth.

"So about my clothes," she said, "what's the problem with them?"

"You need better clothes to have breakfast at the Pacific Room."

She did a double take. "I'm coming to your meeting?"

He eyed her carefully. "Any reason you shouldn't come?"

Her pulse quickened. Sam, her mentor and editor at the *San Francisco Tribune,* had said she was in a unique position to provide some insight into Oakland's mayoral race as Gordon Lee, one of the frontrunners, was Ben's uncle. Sam had also been interested in the Oakland waterfront property that the Lee family planned to redevelop.

At first she had shared Sam's excitement at the opportunity, and she had initially requested Sam dig into Benjamin Lee because she was worried about who she had been sold to. But Ben was nothing like Jake Whitehurst, who had initially bid on her at the Scarlet Auction.

And she had gone undercover to expose the Scarlet Auction, not cover the Lee family.

"No answer, pet?"

That last word snapped her from her thoughts. She decided she liked it better than Slut #2, Jake's moniker for her, but she wasn't sold on being "pet."

She evaded his question by asking, "This is a work meeting, right? About the waterfront property in Oakland?"

"Is that a problem?" He poured two glasses of water and pushed one across the counter in her direction. "Drink."

She raised a brow. "No green tea?"

"Water first. Most people don't drink enough water."

She walked over and took the glass. "Is this part of your control thing? You like to micromanage what people eat and drink?"

"Not always, but when I choose to, I expect you to comply."

The rebel from her teenage years reared its head, but she was wise enough now to know not to fight the smaller battles. She started to drink the water.

"So who's your meeting with?" she asked between sips.

"The head of the Asian Pacific Community Alliance in Oakland. Dawson Chang."

She choked on the water. Of all the people for Ben to be meeting with, did it have to be someone who knew her to be a reporter?

"You okay?" he asked after her coughing fit had settled.

She nodded. "Water went down the wrong pipe."

He was looking at her as if he meant to stare straight through her.

"Is it just you and Dawson Chang?" she asked.

He folded his arms. "Why do you ask?"

"Just curious. It seems rather awkward to bring me to a work meeting. Are you going to pass me off as your assistant or something?"

As much as Sam might have loved for her to be a fly on the wall of a meeting between Benjamin Lee and one of the most influential community leaders in the city, she couldn't risk exposing herself. While Dawson might not remember her from two years ago, when she was a journalism student writing a profile on Carlos De Reyes, the youngest person ever to serve on the city's planning commission and one whom Dawson had mentored, she couldn't take that chance.

"I don't have to pass you off as anything," Ben replied.

"Then how are you going to explain my presence?"

"I don't owe him an explanation."

"But Dawson'll wonder."

He raised a brow. "You're on a first-name basis with him?"

"Well, calling him Mr. Chang sounds rather old-fashioned."

He seemed to buy that. For now.

In researching De Reyes's background, she had come across an old photo of him with Dawson at a noted hangout for the Communist Party. Carlos had admitted to being in the league during his college days and credited Dawson as the biggest influence in his life. According to Carlos, Dawson could do no wrong. She had later interviewed Dawson about Carlos and asked him if he had been a member of the league as well. Dawson had replied, "No comment." At Carlos's request, she had omitted any mention of the league in her write-up.

"What if he thinks I'm your date—or some call girl you picked up?"

He grinned. "Which is worse, the truth or the lie??"

She returned his mocking smile with a scowl. But what if he wasn't joking around? She imagined him commanding her to do something embarrassing—like fetching something in the middle of breakfast. It was one thing to engage in kink-adjacent play in the relative solitude of a cabin in the boondocks of Northern California, and quite another to bring whatever they were doing into a public place in the community where she had grown up.

"I think you'd get a lot more done without me tagging along," she said.

"You're not expected to participate in the meeting."

"Then why have me there?"

"Because I feel like bringing you along."

"You don't trust me to hang out by myself?"

He narrowed his eyes. "Are you trying to be difficult?"

"I'm trying to help you out. And truth be told,

I don't know that I want to sit in a boring developers' meeting."

"You don't strike me as the kind to bore easily," he said. "You strike me as the curious type."

He was assessing her again. She decided to finish her water to show she wasn't trying to be difficult on purpose. What else could she say to persuade him?

"We don't have time to swing by my place to get clothes that would be appropriate for the Pacific Room," she said, even though it wasn't impossible if they hustled.

"I'll take care of it."

"How?"

"My assistant can grab some things from the store."

"No shop is open at this hour."

He turned to his cellphone, which lay on the counter. "Call Beth."

"Good morning, Ben," came a woman's voice after the second ring. "Your reservation is confirmed for the Pacific Room."

"Thank you. I also need reservations for Ishikawa West tonight and to do some clothes shopping for—"

"But I still owe you for the stuff we bought in Weaverville," Kimani protested, refusing to have someone who didn't know her tastes shop for her.

Ben looked her over. "Female in her mid-twenties. Five foot six. About a hundred twenty pounds. Thirty-eight, twenty-six, thirty-six. Size eight shoes."

"Thirty-eight, twenty-eight, thirty-eight" she corrected under her breath, miffed that he had ignored her *and* had her measurements down. She gestured for his attention and whispered, "But I don't want—"

"I need the clothes in time—"

"I don't want or need new clothes," she tried again a little louder.

"—for my meeting with Dawson."

"That doesn't leave me much time," Beth replied, sounding much less fazed than Kimani would have expected.

"Shop fast."

"Shop fast?" Kimani echoed after Ben had hung up. "Even if your assistant could find a shop open this early in the morning, I don't need new clothes."

"Beth is very resourceful. She'll be here. With the clothes."

Partially intrigued at how this was possible, Kimani speculated aloud, "I guess Target could be open this early."

"Beth will probably get Monica to open her boutique early."

She frowned. "Boutique?"

"Monica is a family friend and owns a boutique downtown."

Kimani usually didn't shop the type of stores that could afford the rent downtown.

As if guessing her thoughts, he said, "You don't have to pay for the clothes."

It probably shouldn't matter to her if he wanted to buy her clothes, given that he had "bought" *her*, but she wanted to maintain a little of her dignity. "Look, I know you could probably afford to buy the whole boutique and then some, but I'm not a charity case and I'm not looking for handouts or gifts."

"Who said I'm giving the clothes to you?"

"You don't plan on returning clothes that have been worn?"

He had made two cups of green tea as they spoke. "Of course not."

"Then what will happen to them after I'm done—assuming I wear any of them."

"I'll have Beth donate them to Goodwill."

She couldn't complain about that. Putting aside the issues of the clothes, however, she still had to find a way out of the meeting with Dawson Chang.

"I'm sure your assistant has better things to do than to go shopping for me," she stated. "Like I said, I'd much rather skip your business meeting."

"You'd still need clothes. For dinner tonight. And it's not at a noodle house in Chinatown."

"Doing this Scarlet Auction thing is not something I'd like to broadcast to the world. I'd prefer to keep a low profile during this week, so please don't make me go to this meeting in a public restaurant."

He seemed to take what she said into consideration. To keep him in a better mood, she drank all of her green tea, which surprised her with its crisp aroma. She wasn't much of a tea drinker, but this was easily the best tea she had ever had.

"If you want out of this meeting," Ben said slowly as he eyed her in a way that immediately set her on edge, "you had better ante up."